My Best-Ever Collection of
# FAIRY TALES
# RHYMES &
# BEDTIME STORIES

*An enchanting treasury of*
*145 classic fables for children*

*Retold by Nicola Baxter*

HH
HERMES
HOUSE

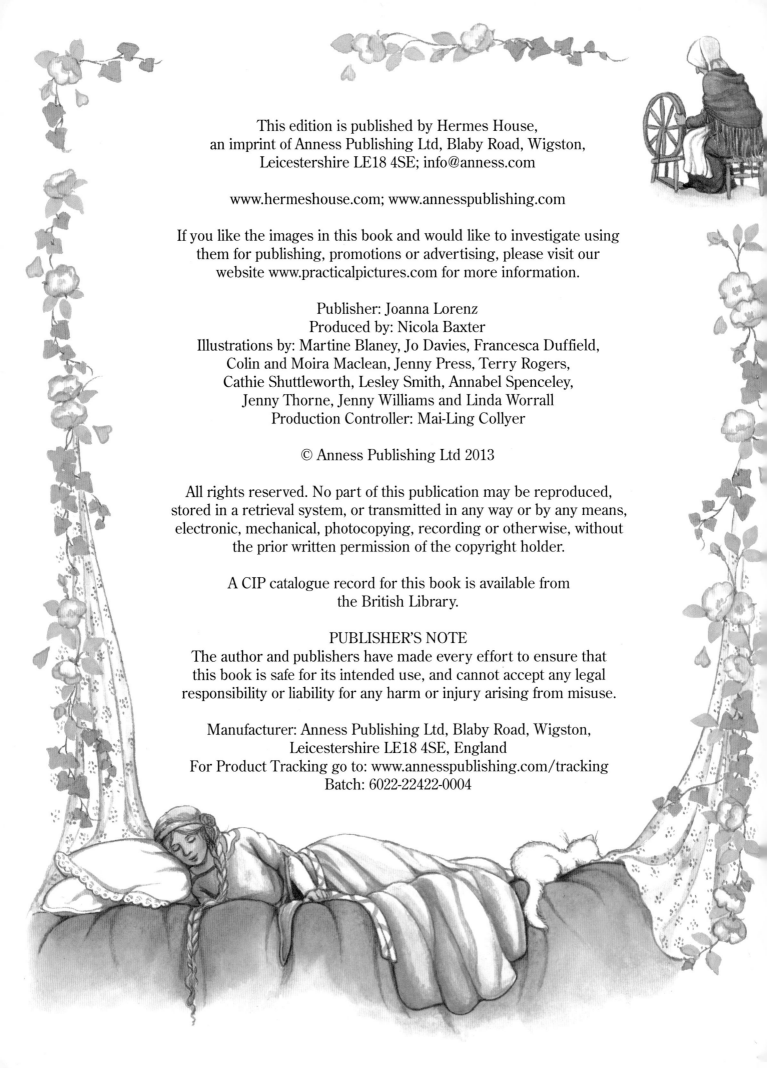

This edition is published by Hermes House,
an imprint of Anness Publishing Ltd, Blaby Road, Wigston,
Leicestershire LE18 4SE; info@anness.com

www.hermeshouse.com; www.annesspublishing.com

If you like the images in this book and would like to investigate using
them for publishing, promotions or advertising, please visit our
website www.practicalpictures.com for more information.

Publisher: Joanna Lorenz
Produced by: Nicola Baxter
Illustrations by: Martine Blaney, Jo Davies, Francesca Duffield,
Colin and Moira Maclean, Jenny Press, Terry Rogers,
Cathie Shuttleworth, Lesley Smith, Annabel Spenceley,
Jenny Thorne, Jenny Williams and Linda Worrall
Production Controller: Mai-Ling Collyer

A CIP catalogue record for this book is available from
the British Library.

PUBLISHER'S NOTE
The author and publishers have made every effort to ensure that
this book is safe for its intended use, and cannot accept any legal
responsibility or liability for any harm or injury arising from misuse.

Manufacturer: Anness Publishing Ltd, Blaby Road, Wigston,
Leicestershire LE18 4SE, England
For Product Tracking go to: www.annesspublishing.com/tracking
Batch: 6022-22422-0004

# Contents

## Teddy Bear Tales

## Fairy Tales

## Animal Tales

# Nursery Rhymes

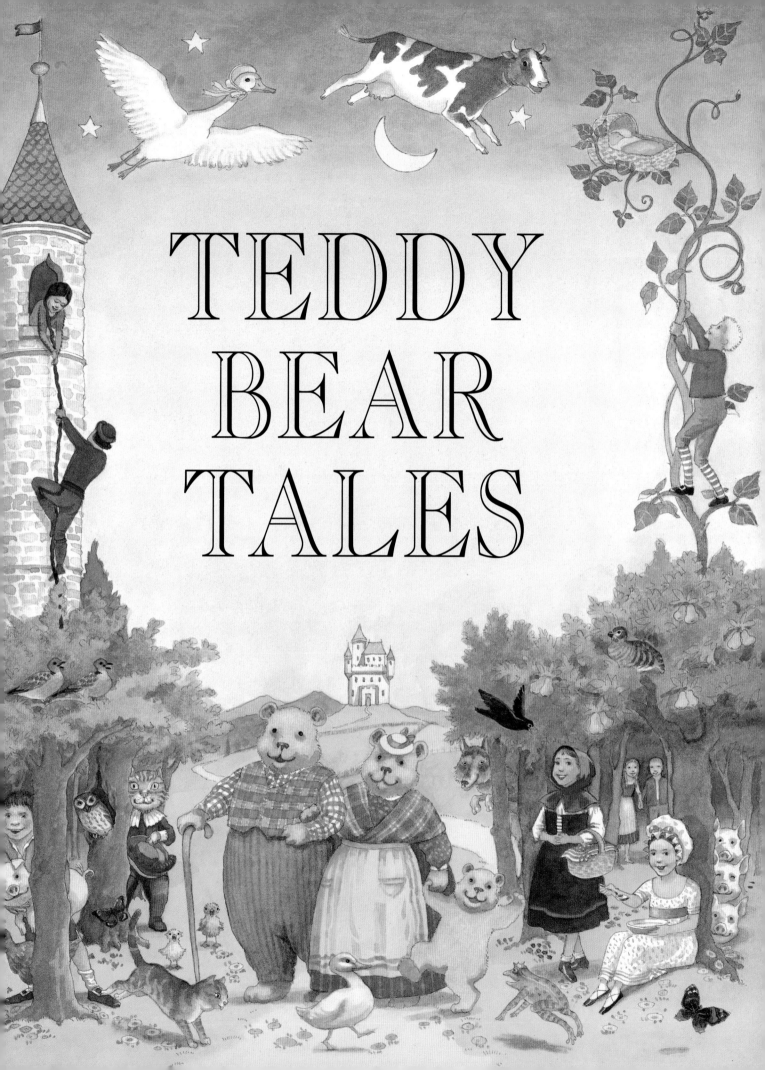

# TEDDY
# BEAR
# TALES

# Ten Little Teddy Bears

Ten little teddy bears
Sitting in a line,
One chased a butterfly
And then there were nine.

Nine little teddy bears
Sitting on a gate,
One fell off it
And then there were eight.

Eight little teddy bears –
Keeping cool is heaven!
One lost his swimming float
And then there were seven.

Seven little teddy bears
Building with some bricks,
One got the hiccups
And then there were six.

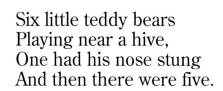

Six little teddy bears
Playing near a hive,
One had his nose stung
And then there were five.

Five little teddy bears
Knocking on the door,
One forgot his present
And then there were four.

Four little teddy bears
Playing by the sea,
One met a giant crab
And then there were three.

Three little teddy bears
Wondering what to do,
One fell fast asleep
And then there were two.

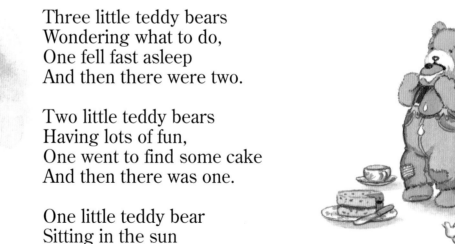

Two little teddy bears
Having lots of fun,
One went to find some cake
And then there was one.

One little teddy bear
Sitting in the sun
Went to find his daddy
And then there were none.

# Goldilocks and the Three Bears

Once upon a time there was a very naughty little girl called Goldilocks. One day when her mother called her to help with the washing up, she pretended not to hear and went off into the woods for a walk instead. This was the kind of thing Goldilocks did quite often.

That day she took a new path and found herself walking past a dainty little cottage. The door of the cottage was slightly open, and naughty Goldilocks simply couldn't resist. The little girl pushed open the door and in she went.

The cottage was as quaint and pretty on the inside as it was on the outside. Goldilocks went into the kitchen and was very pleased to see three bowls of porridge on the table. She was feeling a bit hungry after her walk.

She dipped a spoon into the biggest bowl and tasted the porridge. "Urgh!" she said. "That is far too hot!" The naughty girl spat the porridge out again.

Then she tried the middle-sized bowl. "Urgh!" she cried. "That is far too cold!" You can guess what she did next!

Finally, Goldilocks tried the smallest bowl. She couldn't say anything at all, because she was too busy eating! That porridge was just right.

When she had finished, Goldilocks looked for somewhere to sit down. In the living room were three chairs. Goldilocks sat in the biggest one first, but stood up again. "That chair is far too hard!" she grumbled.

Then the little girl sat down in the middle-sized chair, but she didn't like that one either. "That chair is far too soft!" she complained.

At last Goldilocks sat down in the little chair. It fitted her perfectly. But, oh dear! With a CREAK and a CRACK, Goldilocks landed BUMP on the floor! She was too heavy and the chair had broken into pieces. Goldilocks felt sore in several places!

"I need a rest," muttered Goldilocks, and she climbed up the stairs and into the big bedroom at the top of the house.

There she saw three beds, each with a warm quilt. Goldilocks climbed up onto the largest bed and began jumping up and down. "This will never do! A bed that is too hard to jump on is too hard to sleep on!" she said.

Next she tried the middle-sized bed and curled up in the middle of it, but Goldilocks wasn't comfortable. "It's too soft," she said. "I might sink into it and never be seen again!"

Finally, Goldilocks tried the smallest bed. It was perfect! Before she could think of anything to complain about, Goldilocks was fast asleep.

Now the three bears who lived in the cottage had just gone out for a short walk before breakfast. While Goldilocks slept upstairs, they came back into the kitchen and immediately saw that something was wrong.

"Who's been eating *my* porridge?" asked Father Bear in a growly voice.

"Who's been eating *my* porridge?" asked Mother Bear in a soft voice.

"And who's been eating *my* porridge?" squeaked Baby Bear. "They've eaten it all up!"

Anxiously, the three bears went into the living room.

"Someone's been sitting in *my* chair!" roared Father Bear in a growly voice.

"Someone's been sitting in *my* chair!" cried Mother Bear in a soft voice.

"'And someone's been sitting in *my* chair, and they've broken it into bits!" sobbed Baby Bear.

"Follow me," said Father Bear sternly, and he tiptoed up the stairs.

"Just as I thought," he said. "Someone's been bouncing on *my* bed."

"And someone's been curled up on *my* bed," said Mother Bear.

"And someone's been sleeping in *my* bed," squeaked Baby Bear, "and they're still there! Look!"

At that moment, Goldilocks woke up. She saw three angry, furry faces looking down at her and she jumped out of bed. She ran out of the room and down the stairs and out of the door and into the woods before you could say, "Who's *that?*"

Of course, Goldilocks was careful never to go near the bears' house again. Some people say that she was a good little girl after that, but I'm not so sure about that. Are *you*?

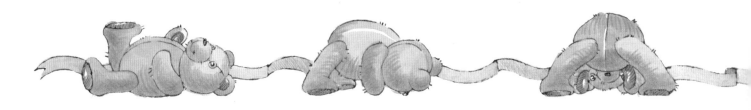

# The Teddy Bear Who Had No Clothes

Teddy Thomson gave a happy little growl. The little girl who was hugging him so tightly was going to be a very good person to live with. He hadn't very much liked being wrapped up in birthday paper, waiting for her to let him out, but now it had all been worth it. Little Katya wouldn't let go of him, even when it was time for her bath.

"But Teddy Thomson's fur will get wet," said her mother. "You can't take him to bed with wet fur. Let me put him here on the laundry basket until you're ready for bed."

Later, Teddy Thomson fell asleep at the end of Katya's little bed, a very happy teddy bear indeed.

But the next morning, when Katya went to school, she had to leave Teddy Thomson behind. At first he was looking forward to meeting the other toys, but no sooner had Katya gone downstairs than he heard them begin to giggle.

"I can hardly look. It's so *embarrassing*!" said the rag doll.

"It shouldn't be allowed!" giggled the baby doll, pointing at Teddy Thomson.

"At least I have paint!" puffed the big blue train, blowing his whistle.

"I feel sorry for him, really," said the clown.

Teddy Thomson couldn't think what they were talking about. He patted his fur and made sure that his paws were clean. At last he couldn't stand it any more. "Excuse me," he rumbled. "'What's the matter with me?"

"My dear, surely you *know?*" gasped the rag doll. "You haven't any clothes on."

"You're a *bare* bear!" chortled the train. "All the toys have their own clothes or bright paint like me. We can't play with you if you don't wear *something.*"

Suddenly Teddy Thomson felt really uncomfortable. None of the bears in the toy store had worn clothes, but now that the others came to mention it, it did seem a bit odd to be bare. "But I haven't *got* any clothes," he said. "And I don't know what teddy bears like me are *supposed* to wear."

The toys didn't want to be unkind, so they tried to find something for him to put on. "Just to start with," they said, "until Katya gives you some clothes."

The rag doll hunted in the toy box. "Here's my best dress," she said. "The one I wear for parties. You can wear it instead."

So Teddy Thomson put on the dress, which really fitted him quite well. But when he looked in the mirror, he could hardly recognize himself among all the pink frills and ribbons.

"Nothing in the world will make me wear this," he said firmly. "If there's one thing I'm sure of, it's that boy bears don't wear dresses." And he took off the rag doll's best party dress and sat down in the corner.

"I've got a spare clown suit," said the clown, helpfully, "and a slightly squashed red nose. You can't wear a clown suit without a red nose."

So Teddy Thomson put on the suit and the nose and went to the mirror again.

"This is even worse!" he cried. "I look ridiculous! You don't see bears with red noses!" Then he pulled off the suit and the red nose and went back to his corner, rubbing his sore face.

"I've got something that suits everyone!" giggled the baby doll, handing Teddy Thomson a square of white material.

"Not in a million years!' growled Teddy Thomson. "I'm a grown-up bear, for goodness sake!"

"Then there's only one thing left," chuffed the train. "We must paint you!" And he chugged off to find Katya's finger paints.

Half an hour later, a rainbow-coloured bear sat sadly in front of the mirror. The toys all told him that he looked *much* better, but he really wasn't sure. "I just hope Katya likes it," he thought. "Because I'm not sure it will *ever* come off!"

When Katya saw Teddy Thomson, she immediately burst into tears. "What's happened to your beautiful golden fur?" she sobbed.

Katya's mother dried her tears and looked thoughtfully at Teddy Thomson. "'I think it's time he *did* have a bath," she said.

So Katya bathed her teddy bear in soapy water and her mother took him outside to dry.

As he slowly dried in the sun, Teddy Thomson made some very important decisions.

"Number one," he said to himself. "It is not dignified for a bear to hang on a washing line by his *ears*. This is not going to happen *ever* again. Number two, I have beautiful golden fur. Katya said so. I'm not going to cover it up with stupid clothes. And I'm going to tell those toys:

> A bear isn't bare
> If he's wearing his fur.
> He's not at his best
> In a clown suit or dress.
> Being covered in paint,
> I'm bound to declare it,
> Was simply not *me*,
> I just couldn't BEAR it!"

# The Big Bad Bear

"You can play wherever you like in the woods," said Mrs. Bear to her twins, "but whatever you do, don't disturb the Big Bad Bear!"

So Lily and Buttons went off to the woods, and at first they were just a little bit frightened. They tiptoed very quietly through the trees. Was that a grumbling, growly noise in the distance? Was that a snorting, snoring sound nearby?

"What is a Big Bad Bear like?" whispered Buttons to his sister.

"Well, he's big and... he's bad... and he's... a kind of bear," said Lily slowly, "and I think I see him over there! Run!"

But when they had finished running, she thought that perhaps she had only seen a bear-shaped bush after all.

The two little bears stood still and listened. Was that a chewing, chomping noise they heard?

"What do Big Bad Bears eat?" asked Lily quietly.

"Oh... berries... and nuts... and insects... and... little bears," said Buttons, "and I think I can hear him coming! Run!"

But when they had finished running, he thought that perhaps it had only been the wind in the branches he had heard after all.

The two little bears tried to play a game, but it was hard to concentrate. Was that a bear's foot poking out from behind a tree? Was that a bear's furry face watching them from between the leaves?

"What does a Big Bad Bear look like?" asked Buttons, looking around rather nervously.

"He is very, very, very tall... and he has very, very, very big teeth... and he has very, very, very long claws," said Lily, "and I think I see him behind that tree! Run!"

But when they had finished running, she thought that perhaps it was only a bird's nest in the branches after all.

Lily and Buttons thought about playing hide and seek. But that would mean being alone. They thought about singing songs. But you-know-who might hear! They wondered if they should start a leaf collection. But if you bend over to pick up a leaf, you just might not see something that's big and bad and bearlike creeping up behind you. So in the end they wandered around and didn't do very much at all.

All of a sudden, Buttons had a very scary thought. He remembered something that he'd heard someone say in a movie once. It seemed horribly true.

"Lily," said Buttons. "I don't like it. It's *too* quiet out here."

Lily listened. The birds weren't singing. The leaves weren't rustling. There were no scampering, scuttling noises at all.

"I don't like it either," she said, "and I think I can see someone coming this way! Run!"

The two little bears ran until they were gasping for breath and could hardly see where they were going. Then... CRASH! They fell over something lying on the ground and landed in a heap under a tree.

Lily peeped out from between her paws and screamed, "Aaaargh!"

Buttons peered around a tree trunk and yelled, "Aaaaargh!"

And the Big Bad Bear looked at them both and shouted, "Aaaaaargh!"

Then they all looked at each other in surprise.

"You're not very big and you don't look very bad," said Lily to the Big Bad Bear.

I'm *not*!" said the little bear indignantly. "That's just my name."

"Then it's a very silly name," said Lily. "Names should be just like the bears they belong to."

The Big Bad Bear gave a big smile. "You're right," he said. "Let's play. But first, tell me what *your* names are…"

23

# Tall Tree Trouble

There is one very important thing to remember if you are going to climb a tree – you have to be able to get down again. It is a pity that Teddy Bellingham didn't think of that before he set out one morning to climb the tallest tree in the garden.

"I sometimes think," said Teddy Bellingham to himself as he clambered up on to the lowest branch, "that people reckon bears aren't very *adventurous*. It's time that a brave, strong bear like me showed them how wrong they are!"

So Teddy Bellingham climbed a little bit farther. It was harder than he had thought it would be when he looked at the tree from the bedroom window. For one thing, the branches didn't seem to be in quite the right places. "This is a badly designed tree, from a climbing point of view," said Teddy Bellingham to himself, as he struggled to reach the next branch.

After climbing a few more branches, tired Teddy Bellingham decided that it was time to have an official rest. In fact, he'd already had a few *unofficial* rests, but they didn't really count. He sat on a branch and swung his legs, then he looked down at the garden.

That was a mistake. When the little bear looked down, he really couldn't help noticing what a *very* long way above the ground he was. "A brave, strong bear who fell off a branch as high as this might hit the ground with a very nasty bump indeed," thought the brave, strong bear in the tree.

Then Teddy Bellingham remembered that climbers always try to look *up* instead of *down*. He held on tight to the trunk and screwed up his eyes. There was still a lot of tree above him. For the first time, Teddy Bellingham wondered if he should have had a little more training for his important tree climb. But he really was a brave bear, and so he carefully began to step on to the next branch.

Teddy Bellingham climbed slowly and steadily. "I'm beginning to get into my stride," he said to himself. "This isn't so difficult after all. The branches seem closer together up here."

It wasn't until his next official rest that Teddy Bellingham noticed that the tree was *moving*. The wind was getting stronger and the tree was swaying gently from side to side. "Ooooh," moaned Teddy Bellingham, holding on very tightly now. "I'm beginning to feel just a little bit queasy." He shut his eyes, but that just made him feel worse. "'Even a brave, strong bear can be ill," he thought. "It wouldn't be wise to go on. I shall climb down carefully and make another attempt tomorrow."

And this was when Teddy Bellingham's troubles *really* began. He found that it is very hard to climb down without *looking* down, and the branches seemed a lot farther apart now. He managed a few branches but then, he had to admit, he was well and truly stuck.

Teddy Bellingham sat on his branch for a very long time. A cold, worried feeling seemed to grow in his tummy. "No one knows I'm here," he thought. "I could stay here for days and days. Or weeks and weeks. Or months and months. Or years and years! My fur will get wet, and my stuffing will fall out, and birds will make nests out of me. Oh, dear!"

But what Teddy Bellingham hadn't noticed was that the branch he was sitting on pointed directly at the house. In fact, its leaves brushed the bedroom window where he often sat.

It wasn't until the sun began to go down, and someone put the light on in the bedroom at the other end of the branch, that Teddy Bellingham realized there was a way to escape.

"I will need to be a braver, stronger bear than I have ever been," he said, "but I think I could *just* reach that bedroom window."

So Teddy Bellingham crawled along the branch. At first it was wide and easy to hold on to, but soon it became narrower. The little bear found that it was safer to wriggle along on his bottom. The nearer he came to the window, the braver he felt. At last he could reach out his paw and *just* touch the window.

It was shut. Teddy Bellingham groaned. But adventurous bears don't give up just like that. He broke off a twig and used it to tap on the window, and through the glass he heard the little boy he lived with talking to someone inside. "Just listen to that tree tapping on the window," the boy said. "It's spooky!"

"It's not spooky, it's *me*!" thought Teddy Bellingham. "How can I show that I'm *not* a tree?"

It was then that Teddy Bellingham had a really good idea. Instead of just tapping with his twig, he made a pattern of the noise. Da, da, da, da-da-da, da, da, da, da-da-da, da, da, da, da-da-da, he tapped. In no time at all, the little boy had opened the window and rescued his teddy bear.

"Of course, I *could* go back and finish climbing that tree today," said Teddy Bellingham to himself the next morning, as he sat comfortably by the window. "But it might become boring if I do it *too* often...."

# The Little Lost Bear

O nce upon a time there was a little teddy bear who kept getting lost. The first time was in the toy store where he was waiting to be bought. Somehow or other, the little bear fell down behind the shelf. By the time he was found, Christmas was over and the shop owner changed her display from bears to one with building sets. So the little bear sat on a shelf in a dark corner of the shop all by himself.

One day, a man came in who was on a business trip. He wanted to take a present home for his little girl, but it had to be something small that he could take on the plane. He couldn't see anything suitable until he noticed the little teddy bear sitting quietly in his dark corner.

"That's just what I need!" cried the man. "Elise has been wanting a little bear like that for ages." He tucked the little teddy bear into his coat pocket and got back into the taxi.

But the traffic on the way to the airport was very heavy, and the man finally arrived only minutes before his plane left.

"Run!" said the lady at the boarding gate. "You may just catch it!" The man ran off down the corridors and fell into his seat just before the doors closed. But when he felt in his pocket for the little teddy bear, he discovered that it had fallen out.

The little bear lay where he had fallen beside the wall. It wasn't until that evening, when the cleaners came along with their wide mops and buckets. that he was found.

"Just look!" said a smiling woman in a blue uniform. "This teddy bear will be perfect for my little nephew. He's coming to stay with me tomorrow." She picked up the little bear and tucked him into one of the big pockets of her uniform.

But the smiling woman was very busy that night. When she got home at last, she threw her uniform into the washing machine without remembering the little bear she had found.

29

Swoosh whoosh! Swoosh whoosh! By the time the washing was emptied out of the machine, the little bear was cleaner than he had ever been in his life! The smiling woman didn't notice him among the clothes. She just left them for her husband to hang out to dry the next day.

In the morning, the smiling woman's husband took the laundry basket out into the garden. But just as he was going to hang out the washing, the telephone rang and he went back inside to answer it. No sooner had he gone, than a naughty puppy came along and carried the little bear off in his mouth.

Puppies love to bury things, and what this puppy wanted more than anything in the world was to dig a big hole and put the little bear in it. But the puppy's owner saw him beginning to dig and cried out, "No, Bouncer! What's that you've got there?"

Bouncer dropped the little bear and ran up to his owner. A minute later, a seagull swooped down and picked up the little bear in its beak. He was carried up above the rooftops and out toward the sea.

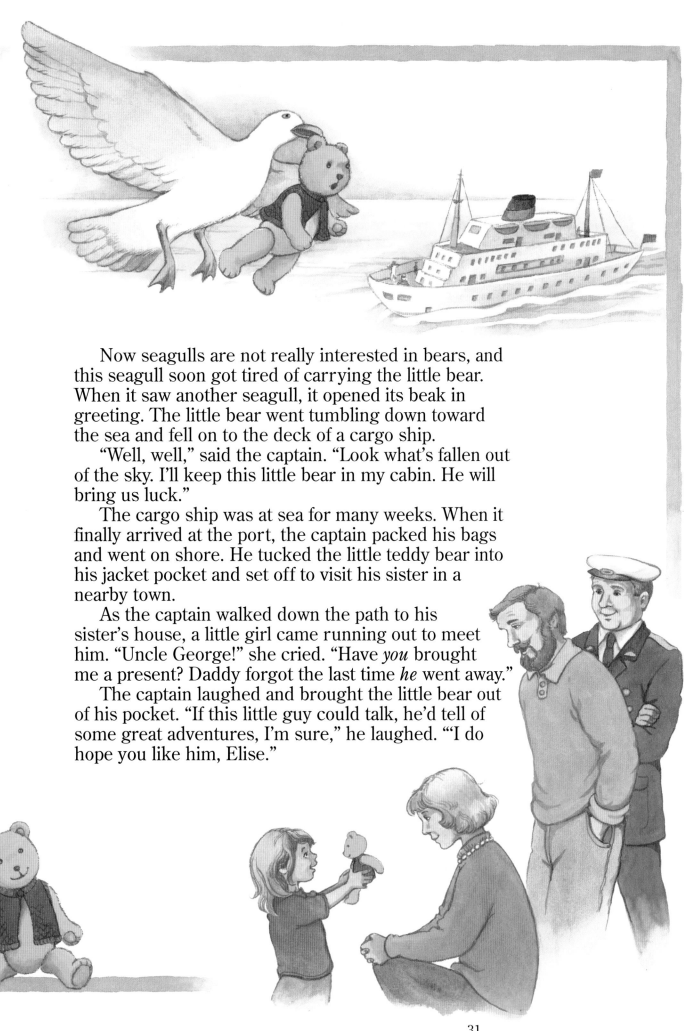

Now seagulls are not really interested in bears, and this seagull soon got tired of carrying the little bear. When it saw another seagull, it opened its beak in greeting. The little bear went tumbling down toward the sea and fell on to the deck of a cargo ship.

"Well, well," said the captain. "Look what's fallen out of the sky. I'll keep this little bear in my cabin. He will bring us luck."

The cargo ship was at sea for many weeks. When it finally arrived at the port, the captain packed his bags and went on shore. He tucked the little teddy bear into his jacket pocket and set off to visit his sister in a nearby town.

As the captain walked down the path to his sister's house, a little girl came running out to meet him. "Uncle George!" she cried. "Have *you* brought me a present? Daddy forgot the last time *he* went away."

The captain laughed and brought the little bear out of his pocket. "If this little guy could talk, he'd tell of some great adventures, I'm sure," he laughed. "'I do hope you like him, Elise."

# There's a Bear in the Bathroom!

"Hey!" yelled Charlie one evening. "There's a bear in the bathroom!"

"Charlie!" shouted his mother. "I've got enough to do looking after the baby, without listening to fanciful stories from you."

The bear smiled at Charlie and turned on the water for him. Then it politely covered its eyes while Charlie undressed and got into the bath.

Charlie looked carefully at the very large bear. There were a lot of questions he wanted to ask, but he chose the most important one. *"What,"* he said, "are you doing in our bathroom?"

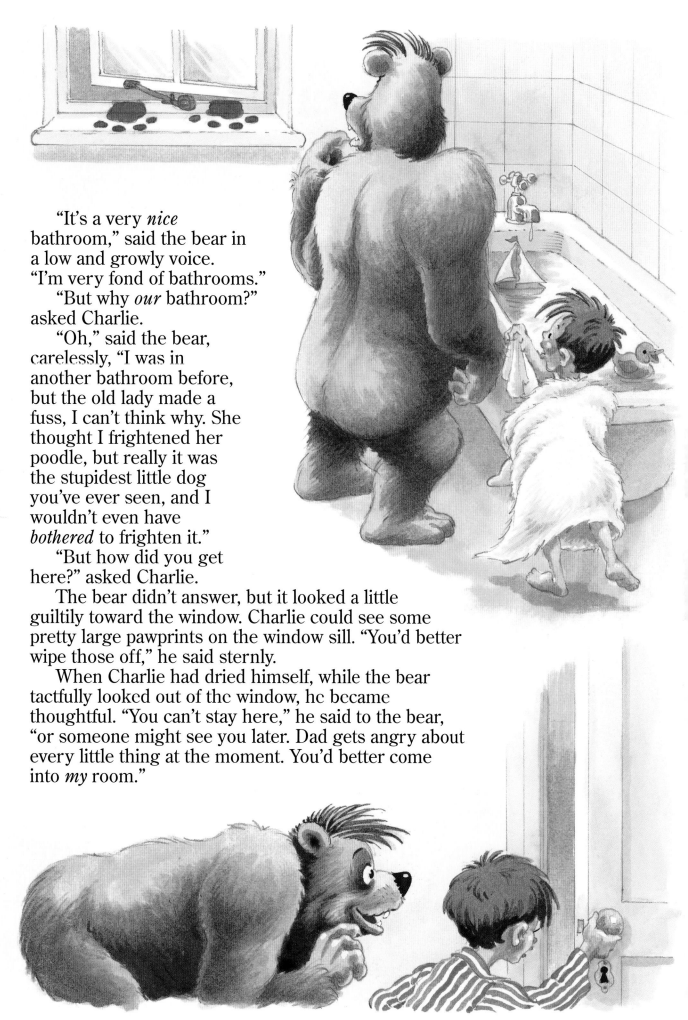

"It's a very *nice* bathroom," said the bear in a low and growly voice. "I'm very fond of bathrooms."

"But why *our* bathroom?" asked Charlie.

"Oh," said the bear, carelessly, "I was in another bathroom before, but the old lady made a fuss, I can't think why. She thought I frightened her poodle, but really it was the stupidest little dog you've ever seen, and I wouldn't even have *bothered* to frighten it."

"But how did you get here?" asked Charlie.

The bear didn't answer, but it looked a little guiltily toward the window. Charlie could see some pretty large pawprints on the window sill. "You'd better wipe those off," he said sternly.

When Charlie had dried himself, while the bear tactfully looked out of the window, he became thoughtful. "You can't stay here," he said to the bear, "or someone might see you later. Dad gets angry about every little thing at the moment. You'd better come into *my* room."

"That's awfully kind of you," said the bear. "I don't suppose you have any... er... little snacks in there, do you?"

Charlie took the bear to his room and gave him a half-eaten bag of soggy potato snacks. The bear ate them happily and Charlie began to see useful possibilities in the horrible carrots that his mother insisted on serving.

"Were you planning to stay long?" he asked the bear as politely as he could.

"Only as long as is convenient," replied the bear. "I thought perhaps you might like some company at the moment."

Charlie sighed. It was true. Ever since his little baby brother had been born a few weeks before, it seemed that no one had any time for *him*. Everything in the house had to do with babies. Relatives came and cooed and gurgled in a ridiculous way.

Charlie did not want to have anything to do with the baby at all. The whole day long it dribbled or cried. If *he'd* done that, he would have been sent up to bed.

"I'm very glad you've come," said Charlie to the bear. "But you're going to have to be very careful not to be found."

"I'll just blend into the background," said the bear.

Charlie was doubtful that anything as big and furry as the bear could "blend" against wallpaper with racing cars on it, but he didn't like to argue.

"Goodnight, bear," he said.

"Goodnight, Charlie," said the bear.

In the morning, Charlie didn't dare to open his eyes. What if he had dreamed it all and the bear wasn't there? But when he opened his eyes, there was the bear smiling at him.

"What are we going to do today?" asked the bear.

Before long, Charlie and the bear became very good friends. They played together all day. The bear was especially good at hide and seek. Although he was a great big bear, he could hide in very tiny places. That was useful when Charlie's mother came in.

"It's not good for you to be all by yourself, Charlie," she said. "Why don't you come and play with your brother? He's crawling around now."

But Charlie didn't like the way that his brother was cuddled all the time. Anyway, he had his own secret friend to play with. "I'm OK here," he said to his mother, but she was already going downstairs because the baby had started to cry.

The bear turned out to be a perfect kind of friend. When Charlie was sad, it gave him a big furry hug. When he was happy, it made funny bear-faces that made Charlie laugh so much, his tummy ached.

One day, Charlie went downstairs to find some apples for the bear and got quite a surprise. In the living room, his little brother was standing up holding on to the arm of a chair. He looked up, smiling all over his little face, and said, "Charlie!"

Charlie looked down. The little kid really wasn't so bad at all, and he liked the idea of being a big brother. Charlie bent down and looked carefully at the little boy, who had let go of the chair with his chubby hands and was tottering toward Charlie. Then he fell forward and held on to Charlie's knees.

Charlie sat on the floor and helped his little brother to stand up. He was even warmer and cuddlier than the bear and he smiled up at Charlie with a friendly little face. Charlie forgot all about food for the bear and played until suppertime.

That night Charlie helped his mother to put his little brother to bed. "Thanks for all your help today, Charlie," she said, giving him a hug. "We've missed not having you around."

When Charlie went to bed, he thought for a minute about telling the bear all about his little brother. But he wasn't very surprised to find that the bear was nowhere to be seen, and there were big black pawprints on the window sill.

# The Horrible Hat

"Please," begged Little Bear, "don't wear that hat."

It was Parents' Day at Little Bear's school and his mother was getting ready.

"Don't be silly, Little Bear," she said, picking up the big purple and orange hat. "It's a beautiful hat."

Little Bear hid his face in his paws. She was going to do it *again*. It seemed to Little Bear that his mother did her best to embarrass him on every occasion. Nobody else's mother would be wearing a purple and orange hat. Probably nobody else's mother would be wearing a hat *at all*. He tried one more time.

"It's awfully windy," he said. "Your hat might blow off and... and... fall in the river."

His mother looked down with a frown. "Little Bear, you're not making sense. We won't be anywhere *near* the river. Now come along. It's time we went."

Little Bear followed his mother miserably to the car. There was hardly room in it for Little Bear *and* his mother *and* the hat. Dangling feathers tickled his nose all the way to the school.

Other parents were walking toward the gates as Mrs. Bear stopped under a tree. Little Bear was relieved to see that some mothers were wearing hats. But not very many. And they were very small hats! When Mrs. Bear got out of the car, everybody turned to look at her. Little Bear wished he was even smaller. He wanted to curl up and never see any of his friends ever again. But his mother was striding toward the school, calling and waving.

Inside the school, he felt even worse. The hat had seemed very big and bright at home. It had seemed even bigger and brighter in the car. But now in the classroom, as she bent over his desk to look at his model skyscraper, it almost seemed to *glow.* "She might as well have a flashing light on her head," thought Little Bear.

Little Bear did the only thing he could. He wandered farther and farther away from where his mother was talking to a teacher, and then hurried off to hide in the cloakroom. "I hope I'm never found," he said to himself miserably.

In another room, something happened that nearly made his wish come true. Old Boffin Bear, who helped in science lessons, was showing an experiment to some parents when something went horribly wrong. Instead of the puff of green smoke that he had been hoping for, there was a burst of orange flame. The next minute little flames were dancing along the desk and on to the floor.

"Fire!" yelled Old Boffin Bear. "Everybody out! Oh my goodness! Oh my goodness! Keep calm everyone! Oh my goodness! Follow me!"

There was terrible confusion. White smoke swirled out of the room and down the hallways. Soon everyone knew that there was a fire. "Please walk to the exits," called Little Bear's teacher. "They are lit up in green. You can see them through the smoke. There's no need to panic."

In a matter of seconds everyone was safely in the playground. Well, *almost* everyone. "Where's Little Bear?" cried Little Bear's mother. "I'm going back in!"

"Stop!" cried the teacher, but there was no stopping Mrs. Bear. The rooms were filled with smoke, but she found that there was a little gap of clear air near the floor. So she crawled on her hands and knees, calling, "Little Bear, where are you?"

Little Bear had heard the confusion and seen the smoke come swirling toward him, but he was too small to see the exit signs. He crouched in the cloakroom, feeling more afraid than he had ever been in his life. Then he thought he saw something moving through the smoke. It was something that glowed orange. The fire was coming this way! But as Little Bear watched, he saw that the orange thing was round and, yes, it had purple dangly bits all around. Never in his life had Little Bear been so pleased to see the horrible orange and purple hat. "Oh, Little Bear!" cried his mother. "I'm so glad to have found you. Come on, this is the way out."

When Little Bear and his mother appeared in the playground, everyone clapped and cheered. The firefighters arrived and found that it was only a small fire that had made lots of smoke. "So all's well that ends well," said Little Bear's teacher. "Except for your lovely hat, I'm afraid, Mrs. Bear."

It was true. Little Bear's mother's hat was blackened by smoke and the edges were drooping. "Don't worry," said Little Bear, giving her a big hug. "I'm going to save up and buy you an even *bigger* hat. Just you wait and see!"

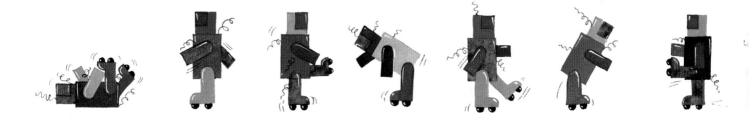

# The Most Beautiful Bear

"**I** am the most beautiful teddy bear in the world," thought Mopsybell. She could just see her reflection in the shop window. Her golden brown fur was fluffy. Her paws were pink and clean. Her eyes were bright and shiny. She was sure that the next little girl to come into the shop would choose her. "She'll love me and look after me and keep me safe and warm," thought Mopsybell. "And I'll live in the kind of house that is just right for a beautiful bear like me."

Just then a little girl *did* come into the shop with her grandmother.

"Now, Juliette," said Grandma. "You may choose whichever teddy bear you like best as a special present. I'm surprised that no one has bought you a bear before, but luckily I can put that right. Every little girl should have a teddy bear of her own."

The little girl scowled. "I don't really like bears," she said. "They're for babies. I'd much rather have a robot."

"Don't be silly, dear," said Grandma. "You can't cuddle a robot. Now, which bear would you like? What about that big beautiful one in the window?"

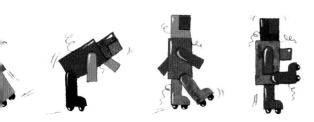

Mopsybell wriggled on her shelf. Just as she had expected, she was going to be chosen. But the little girl groaned.

"That's the most stupid-looking bear I've ever seen," she said. "Look at that silly pink bow around its neck. It's hideous."

Mopsybell was so shocked, she nearly fell off the shelf. Hideous? Her? What a horrible child!

Grandma was determined. "If you don't like that bear, dear, choose another one," she said, "but be quick."

Instead, Juliette was looking at a model dinosaur with huge teeth. "I'd rather have this," she said. "It reminds me of *you*, Grandma."

Grandma smiled nervously at the shop assistant. "Now," she said. "What about this little pink bear?"

Juliette had wandered further into the shop. "Pink?" she yelled. "I might be sick. Couldn't I have this Dracula outfit? That reminds me of..."

"Juliette!" said Grandma quickly, "I've made up my mind. I know you'll love this bear when you get her home, and she'll always remind you of me. Now put those spiders down, dear, and let's go home."

The shop assistant took Mopsybell off the shelf and gave her to the little girl. Juliette took hold of Mopsybell's ear and dragged her along the ground. "Not like that," cried Grandma. "You'll make her beautiful fur dirty. Let me carry her."

"I am still the most beautiful bear in the world," thought Mopsybell as they went home on the bus. "Juliette will know that as soon as she has taken a good look at me."

Sure enough, when Grandma had taken Juliette home and hurried off to catch her train, the little girl took a long hard look at her bear. "I can think of some uses for you after all," she said in a rather odd tone.

All too soon, Mopsybell found out what she had meant. Mopsybell was just the right size for Juliette's parachute experiments. Tied to a pillow case, she was dropped out of every upstairs window in the house. Once she was very nearly lost for ever, and it was only luck that Juliette's mother found her.

Then Juliette decided to start growing things. She spent ages digging in the garden and watching worms. Then she sprinkled some seeds on the ground and tied Mopsybell to a post nearby.

"I found your bear in the garden, Juliette," said her mother that night. "You must have forgotten her."

"No," explained Juliette. "She's a scarecrow, keeping the birds away from my seeds."

"A scarecrow! I shall die of shame," thought Mopsybell. "Thank goodness the other bears in the shop can't see me now."

Over the weeks that followed, Mopsybell was wrapped up like an Egyptian mummy, pulled along on a piece of string to see if she would fly like a kite, and dropped in the pond when Juliette looked for tadpoles.

Just when Mopsybell was seriously thinking about running away, Juliette had to have her tonsils taken out and went into the hospital. Lying in bed, as her sore throat got better, Juliette found that she missed Mopsybell. "She's a very silly bear," she thought to herself. "But I do *need* an assistant for my experiments. And she's quite cuddly too."

So Mopsybell was brought to the hospital and snuggled down in Juliette's bed. "At last she realizes how beautiful I am," thought Mopsybell. "Now I'll be looked after as I should be. Anyway, things couldn't be *worse* than they were."

It was lucky that Mopsybell couldn't hear what Juliette was thinking as she cuddled her bear closer. "I'm going to look after you and make sure you're never ill, Mops," she promised, "because I'm going to be a famous doctor when I grow up. Now I wonder who I could use for my operating practice?"

# Mr. Bear's New House

Doo, da, doo, dee dum, dum. "I've never heard such a dreadful noise," groaned Mr. Bear, pulling his quilt up over his ears. "How am I ever going to get any sleep?" The bear in the next house was playing his drums again. "It was bad enough when he learned to yodel," thought Mr. Bear. "And when he started to learn the trumpet, it was *awful*. But this drumming is the worst so far. It's loud and he's *hopeless* at it. There's only one answer. I'm going to have to move."

The next morning, bright and early, Mr. Bear set out to find another house. The first one he looked at seemed perfect. It was in a quiet lane, with a big garden at the back. Sunshine streamed into the rooms, and the house felt friendly and warm. Mr. Bear was about to say, "I'll take it!'" when the house began a strange sort of shivering and shaking. The chairs wobbled. The lampshades tinkled. The doors rattled in their frames.

"It's an earthquake!" cried Mr. Bear, throwing himself under the table.

The agent who was showing Mr. Bear around got down on his hands and knees. "Er... I don't know if I happened to mention that this property is very close to the train station?" he said.

"A little *too* close for my liking," replied Mr. Bear, as soon as his heart had stopped pounding.

The next house seemed much better. It stood on a hill with a garden all around it. Mr. Bear could see that there were no trains for miles around. The rooms were small and simple. It was just right for a bear who wanted a quiet life. Mr. Bear opened his mouth to say that he would like to move in, but his words were drowned out by a screaming, roaring, rushing overhead.

"Sorry,'" said the agent, "I didn't hear you. The low-flying exercises that the planes do over these hills are a bit noisy, aren't they? But it's only a few times a day."

"A few is too many for me," said Mr. Bear firmly. "Isn't there anywhere you can show me that is far away from trains or planes or any kind of noise?"

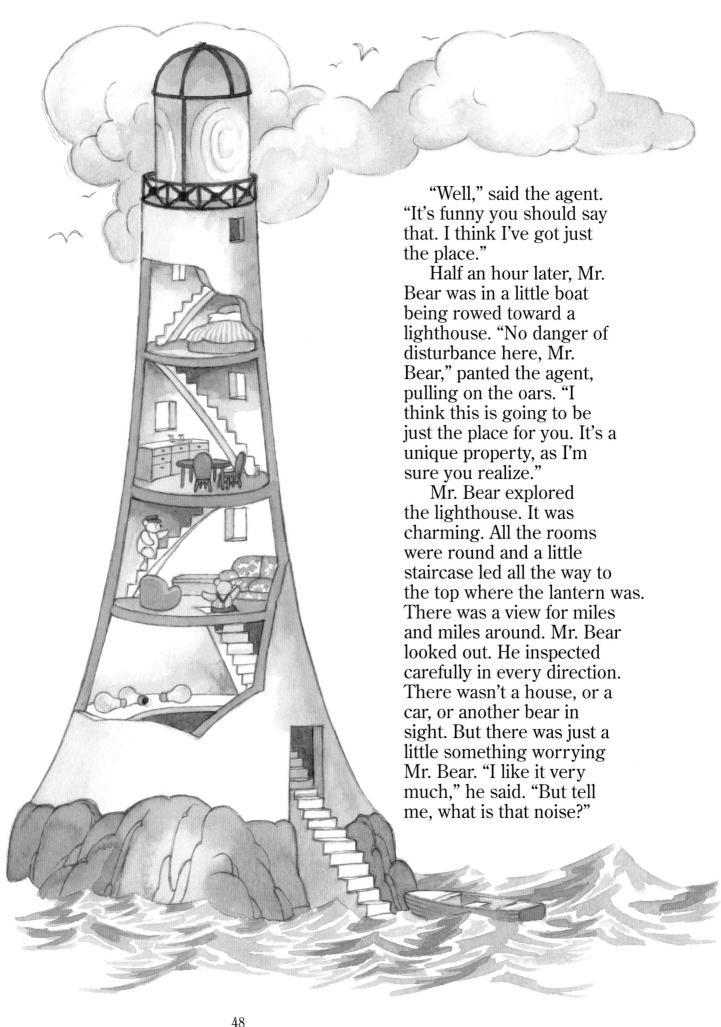

"Well," said the agent. "It's funny you should say that. I think I've got just the place."

Half an hour later, Mr. Bear was in a little boat being rowed toward a lighthouse. "No danger of disturbance here, Mr. Bear," panted the agent, pulling on the oars. "I think this is going to be just the place for you. It's a unique property, as I'm sure you realize."

Mr. Bear explored the lighthouse. It was charming. All the rooms were round and a little staircase led all the way to the top where the lantern was. There was a view for miles and miles around. Mr. Bear looked out. He inspected carefully in every direction. There wasn't a house, or a car, or another bear in sight. But there was just a little something worrying Mr. Bear. "I like it very much," he said. "But tell me, what is that noise?"

"'Noise? What noise?" asked the agent.

"*That* noise," said Mr. Bear. "Listen. It's a sighing, coming-and-going, swooshing sort of a noise."

The agent listened hard. "I can't hear anything at all," he said. "Except the sea, of course,"

"Ah," said Mr. Bear. "The sea. I suppose that goes on *all* the time?"

"Well, yes," said the agent. "Er... it's all around you."

Mr. Bear thanked the agent for his time and made his way home. No sooner had he settled down with a mug of cocoa and a book, when the drumming next door started up again. Mr. Bear looked up from his reading for a moment and smiled. "I do believe he's improving," he said.

# The Exciting Life of Uncle Bobo

"So you want to be a pilot, my lad?" said Uncle Bobo to his nephew, Henry Bear. "Ah, how well I remember my first days at the controls of an S29 plane. Of course, in those days we didn't have proper training. Pilots today don't know how lucky they are. Then, they put you in the cockpit, told you what the dials meant, and let you go.

I had some hair-raising experiences, I can tell you. I'll never forget flying through the blue one Saturday afternoon, the sun glinting on my goggles, and looping the loop over your grandmother's house. I was flying so low that some of her laundry got caught on the tail, and I flew all the way back to base with a pair of your grandfather's long johns flying out behind! He was *furious,* but we laughed about it together later."

"Gosh," said Henry. He began to think that maybe he wouldn't be a pilot after all. It would be hard to live up to Uncle Bobo's adventures. It would be much, much better to do something that no one in the family had ever done before. "I've decided to be a chef when I grow up," he announced.

"Ah, a chef?" said Uncle Bobo, when next he visited. "Did I ever tell you about the time I was personal chef to Prince Bruinski? Many's the time I've cooked a banquet for five thousand people with only one assistant to hand me my whisks. I remember the time the King of Oursania fell headlong into one of my giant cakes. It took them three days to find him, but when they did, he was beaming all over his face and saying, 'Maestro, that was the finest cake I ever had the good fortune to fall into.' How we all laughed!"

"Goodness," said Henry. It would be hard to find a Prince these days, he thought. And the idea of cooking for thousands was a bit alarming. Some days it was hard enough to open the cereal box without pouring the contents all over his feet! Perhaps being a chef wasn't such a good idea after all. Henry watched an ant scurrying along the floor and rushed off to look in the dictionary. "I'm going to be an ent-o-mol-o-gist," he told his family. They looked at him blankly. "It's someone who knows about insects," he explained.

A few days later, there was a postcard from Uncle Bobo. On the front was a picture of a tropical forest with huge red flowers and a snake in one corner. Henry read the card with a sinking feeling in his tummy. "Dear Henry," it said. "Just a few lines from my entomological study tour of Brazil. This morning I discovered three species of giant ant previously unknown to bear. One of my assistants was carried off yesterday by a mammoth elephant moth! Poor bear. How would you like to be my assistant on my next trip? Best wishes, Uncle Bobo."

Henry sighed. There must be *something* that Uncle Bobo wasn't an expert at. He thought long and hard. By the time Uncle Bobo came to his birthday party, he had decided. "When I grow up," he announced, "I'm going to be the most famous Henry in the world." And he looked at Uncle Bobo with a triumphant smile.

But Uncle Bobo didn't hesitate for a second. "Goodness me, young Henry," he said. "How you take me back. It seems only yesterday that I changed my name to Bobo. I had to, you see. I was so well known that I couldn't walk down the street without being

mobbed by my fans. I didn't mind too much, but it was very hard for your Aunt Hilda. I admit, I was touched when your parents decided to call you Henry after me. And now you're going to follow in my footsteps. Well, well, well."

Henry just wanted to crawl under the table and disappear. Tears came to his eyes. He hoped that he would never, ever have to grow up after all, but then there was a chuckle from the other side of the room.

"Don't tease the poor little bear, Bobo," said Aunt Hilda. "You've only had one job in your life and you know it. Tell Henry what you do."

"I'm sorry, Henry," said Uncle Bobo. "Can't you guess? I'm a writer. I make up stories for children just like you. And they could be about anything you can think of... even myself!"

Henry looked at Uncle Bobo and slowly began to understand. "So you weren't a pilot, or a chef, or an ent-o-mot-o-gist?" he said. Suddenly, he began to feel a lot better. "When *I'm* grown up," he said. "I'm going to be a writer. And I may have a lot to say ahout *uncles.*"

# Bears Everywhere

Joseph was the easiest boy in the world to please. He liked *anything* as long as it had bears on it. He had bears on his slippers and bears on his socks. His bedroom curtains had bear pawprints all over them. He had a whole shelf full of stories about bears, and on his bed sat his own special teddy bear, Rufus.

Joe loved Rufus best of all. He told the old bear all his secrets and all his worries. And Rufus seemed to understand. At night, Joe propped Rufus up beside him on his pillow. Even when it was very, very dark, Rufus made sure that nothing really bad happened.

One day Joe's cousin Kelly asked him to visit. "You are lucky," said Katy, Joe's big sister. "She lives on a farm and there's lots to do. I wish I was going too."

"You can help Joe to pack, Katy," said her mother. "You know that you *would* have been invited if you hadn't put gravy in Aunt Susan's handbag."

Katy grumbled all the time as she helped to put Joe's clothes in his case. "It was just a joke," she said. "How was I to know she'd hold it upside down when she opened it? Joe, what are you *doing*?"

"I'm putting Rufus in," said Joe. "He doesn't really like being inside, but I'm afraid he might get lost on the train otherwise."

"But you can't take *Rufus*!" laughed Katy. "Everyone will think you're a real baby. Baby Joe, Baby Joe, has to take his teddy bear!"

Joe stood still for a moment. "But I have to take Rufus," he said, with tears in his eyes.

Somehow that just made Katy even meaner. "Look, Joe," she said, "we don't say anything at home, because we *know* you. But trust me, no one who is nearly five takes a teddy bear around with him. They'll never stop laughing at the farm. And you'd better leave those slippers behind as well."

Joe became very red. He ran down to his mother. "I've decided not to go to Kelly's after all," he said.

"Joe, it's far too late to change your mind," said his mother. "Bring your suitcase downstairs. Aunt Susan will be here any minute."

So Joe went up and got his little suitcase. Rufus sat on the bed and looked at him with a sad look in his beady eyes. Joe couldn't stand it. But just then, Katy

walked past the door. "Baby Joe, Baby Joe," she sang softly. Joe put Rufus back on the bed and went downstairs. He felt a cold empty space in his tummy.

Later on, in the train with Aunt Susan, he almost forgot about Rufus, and it was exciting seeing the farm and all the animals. Kelly showed him her playroom and all her toys. "You can play with any of them you like," she offered.

Joe looked around. "Haven't you got a teddy bear?" he asked. "Oh, no," said Kelly. "I like cars best. You can't race a teddy bear."

Joe thought about crawling races he had had with Rufus in the hall, but he didn't say anything. He was very quiet as they had supper.

"I expect you're tired," said Aunt Susan, looking at his pale face. "Finish your ice cream and I'll come and tuck you in."

Joe lay very still in the strange bedroom opposite Kelly's. There were roses on the wallpaper. As the room became darker, they started to look like ogres' faces, with big staring eyes and grimacing mouths. He buried his face in the pillow but he could still see the faces, even with his eyes shut.

"Oh Rufus," thought Joe, "I do wish you were here."

During the day, Joe could sometimes almost forget that he was sad, but he just couldn't get to sleep in the room with the ogres' faces.

Aunt Susan became very worried. "He won't tell *me* what's the matter," she said to her husband. "Why don't you have a talk with him?"

Uncle Richard went up and sat on Joe's bed. "What's the matter, old boy?" he asked. "Missing your mother?"

Joe shook his head.

"Your dad? Katy?"

Joe shook his head again. Without realizing he was doing it, he patted the pillow where Rufus usually sat.

"You know," said Uncle Richard. "When I used to stay with my Granny, I never felt homesick because I took my old bear, Mr. Bumble, with me. He was my best friend."

Then Joe told Uncle Richard all about Rufus and how much he missed him. Uncle Richard smiled. "I understand, old man," he said. "I'm afraid I can't get Rufus for you, but I guess I could get along without Mr. Bumble for a night or two, if you'd like to borrow him."

Joe opened his eyes wide. "But you're older than *five!*" he said.

"Just a bit," grinned Uncle Richard. "What has someone been saying? Just between you and me, Joe, I feel rather sorry for people who don't understand about bears, don't you?"

# Grandfather Bear
# Goes Fishing

"I'll be back this evening, dear," said Grandfather Bear to Grandmother Bear. "I'm going to have a nice quiet day fishing down by the river."

"Why you want to go sitting around on chilly riverbanks at your age, I'll never know," grumbled his wife. "You'll catch a dreadful cold and who will have to run up and down stairs bringing you honey and lemon or soup? I will! I don't know why you can't just sit in your chair and read the paper like other bears."

"I'll wear my warmest coat, dear," murmured Grandfather Bear, hurrying out of the door. He was looking forward to a long, peaceful day, sitting on the riverbank and dreaming of the great big fish that would one day be nibbling at his line.

It was a beautiful day and Grandfather Bear hummed to himself as he strolled along the bank, looking for a good place to sit. At last he found just the spot. It was sheltered by bushes so that passing bears would not see him and disturb him with chatter.

"This is my idea of a perfect day," said Grandfather Bear to himself as he set up his little fishing stool. "Peace and quiet at last."

But five minutes later, someone coughed loudly behind him. Grandfather Bear nearly jumped out of his skin. "It's only me," said little Bruno Bear, who lived down the road. "Mrs. Bear was worried your ears would get cold, so she asked me to bring your hat."

Grandfather Bear couldn't be angry with young Bruno. "Thank you very much," he said. "Tell her I'll put it on immediately. Now you run along and play."

Grandfather Bear settled down again. He did feel snug and warm in the woolly hat. But just as he was drifting off into a daydream about having his picture in the Fishing Gazette, a voice shouted in his ear, "How are you, old fellow?"

"There's no need to shout," cried Grandfather Bear, seeing his friend from next door.

"Your wife asked me to bring your scarf," explained the friend. "It *is* rather chilly today. Let me wrap it around your neck for you."

"It's all right," said Grandfather Bear a little irritably. "I can do it myself. Thanks very much, though."

The bear from next door went on his way. In the trees along the riverbank, the birds began to sing. Grandfather Bear took a deep breath of country air. "This is the life," he thought. All at once, a horrible noise shattered the peace of the riverbank.

It was Grandfather Bear's nephew on his motorbike. "What are you doing?" cried the old bear in dismay. "You can't bring that machine here."

"Sorry," said his nephew. "But Aunty was sure you would need a hot snack about this time of the morning. I brought it as fast as I could so that it wouldn't get cold before I got here. It's toasted sandwiches, I think."

Grandfather Bear sighed. He could smell the sandwiches in the box his nephew was holding out. Come to think of it, he did feel a little bit empty somewhere beneath his third waistcoat button. "Thanks very much," he said. "Now take that noisy machine away. You're frightening the fish."

Alone again, Grandfather Bear munched into his sandwiches. They were delicious. When he had eaten them, he felt full and warm and happy. He settled down for a little snooze after his snack.

It seemed only seconds later that he felt a hand on his shoulder. "Mr. Bear! Are you all right?" It was Maisie, who worked in the Post Office.

"I'm fine," said Grandfather Bear. "What are you doing here, Maisie?"

"Oh," said Maisie. "Mrs. Bear knows that I always take a walk along the river at lunchtime and she asked me to bring you this flask of coffee."

"Thank you," said Grandfather Bear weakly. "That's very kind," and Maisie went on her way.

Grandfather Bear took a drink of coffee. It was just as he liked it. He sipped the coffee and watched a leaf floating down the river, and felt very contented. The honking of a bicycle horn disturbed his thoughts.

"I just don't believe it," muttered Grandfather Bear. "I might as well sit in the middle of Main Street."

On the bicycle was Fred from the garage. "I'm on my way home," he said, "and your wife asked me to bring you your gloves. You can't be too careful, even on a day like this."

"That *is* kind," said Grandfather Bear. "But I was just about to pack up and go home. Thank you for your trouble, though."

"I'm home, dear," called the old bear as he walked into the hall. Grandmother Bear hurried to meet him. "Have you had a good day? Did you catch anything?"

Grandfather Bear raised his eyes to the ceiling. "No, dear," he smiled. "Not even a cold!"

# Harold Hubertus Bear

Harold Hubertus Bear, HH to his friends, was no ordinary bear. His great-grandmother had been a Princess among the royal Russian bears. His mother came from a long line of bears who had rubbed paws with Dukes and Countesses. In fact, he was a very well-connected bear indeed.

HH was a kind bear and many people were very fond of him, but he did tend to put on airs. "It just isn't *proper* to wear a red bowtie in the morning," he would say, shaking his head, when he met another bear in the street. "Blue or black only for the mornings, dear bear. We mustn't let standards drop."

In fact there was very little happening in Bearport that Harold Hubertus didn't wish to express an opinion about. "Of course, I am always consulted," he would say. "Other bears know that when it comes to matters of importance, you need a bear who has seen a bit of the world and mixed with the right sort."

Now as far as anyone knew, Harold Hubertus had only ever been as far as the seaside on a hot Saturday in summer. It was true that he was sometimes invited to weddings and christenings of distant relations with titles to their names, but none had ever been seen visiting HH at Humpleton Hall. This was what made it particularly annoying when Harold Hubertus boasted about his friends. "As I was saying to the Duchess only the other day..." or, "I know that Her Royal Highness agrees with me..." he would say.

"It's high time that bear came back down to earth," said Mr. Bloomer, the baker. "Any ideas, Basil?" Basil, his nephew, shook his head, but he looked thoughtful.

A few weeks later, the whole town was buzzing with news. Princess Ursula Berelli was coming to visit Harold Hubertus.

"Is she a relative of yours?" Mr. Bloomer asked HH when he came into the bakery for special cakes.

"Er... well, I believe... er... ours is a very big family, you know," said HH. "She's a rather distant... er... cousin, I think."

Harold Hubertus worked night and day to make sure that the visit would be a success. He had several rooms in the Hall redecorated. He had six extra gardeners working on the lawns, just in case the Princess wanted to take a stroll. For weeks, he planned menus and entertainment, choosing the most delicious and the most expensive foods and outings. By the time the great day arrived, HH was exhausted.

At the agreed time, Harold Hubertus had all the servants line up on the steps of the Hall. He had seen this in a film and thought it looked impressive. The sound of an engine could be heard coming down the main street. A very small car swept through the gates of the Hall and up to the front door.

Harold Hubertus was amazed. But perhaps the Princess had sent on some servants ahead? No, when the car door opened, out stepped someone who was undoubledly a Princess. Well, she wore a little crown on her head and a few more jewels than Harold Hubertus had been used to thinking was quite right in the daytime.

Nevertheless, he stepped forward to greet her with a deep bow and gallantly kissed the paw she held out to him.

"My dear Princess," said HH, "has your car broken down?"

The Princess roared with laughter. "You dear, old-fashioned thing!" she shrieked. "Nobody who is *anybody* is driving a large car nowadays. Think of the environment, Humblebus."

"Quite so, quite so," said her host. "It's Harold Hubertus, actually. Won't you come into the Hall? You must need a snack after your journey."

The Princess allowed herself to be led into the dining room, where the tables were piled high with a huge range of dishes. The Princess allowed her eyes to linger for a minute on a particularly fine-looking dessert before she said, "Dear Horribilus, I'm afraid I never touch anything richer than a slice of toast and a morsel of cheese. Why not give this wonderful food to the people of the town?"

"What a charming idea," said HH with a gulp. "I'll tell the servants to take it away at once. And... er... it's Harold Hubertus."

"A thousand apologies, Hardboiledus," cried the Princess. "But tell me, are you really so behind the times as to have servants? I can hardly believe it."

"Er... that sort of thing is no longer done, I suppose, in your circle?" enquired HH in a shaky voice.

"Goodness me, no, Hurglegurglus," laughed the Princess. "I'm sure, like me, that you would much prefer to do your own cooking and cleaning. It's so much more modern."

"Yes, yes," said Harold Hubertus. "But it's hard to change things so quickly in the country."

"Then you must make a start yourself, Humpus Dumpus," said the Princess. "I will come with you and help you to take all this delicious food to the good townspeople. Roll up your sleeves now!"

It was not until the end of a long and very tiring day, after the Princess had forced Harold Hubertus to carry plates of food with his own hands to every inhabitant of Bearport, that HH suddenly noticed something about the Princess that he had not noticed before. She was wearing a bracelet around her wrist that read, quite clearly, *Basil*.

Delicately he pointed it out to the Princess. "Ah," she cried, "a herb I adore! Now it really is time for me to go." And she swept outside and into her little car.

Harold Hubertus walked slowly home and thought about the events of the day. As he walked, old and young bears stopped to shake his hand and thank him for his generosity.

"I fear," said Harold Hubertus to himself, "that I have been a very foolish old bear. But everyone else is happy, and that makes me happy too. And only a bear with real pedigree can take a joke as well as I can, after all."

# The Trouble with Edward

"Where's that bear?" roared Mr. Teddington from the garage. "Someone – and I think I know who – has filled my boots with mud!"

Edward put his head around the garage door and tried to explain. "I was trying to start a wormery, Dad. We've been learning about worms at school, but your boots weren't very good for a wormery because I couldn't see through them."

"Oh, excuse *me,*" said his father sarcastically. "Next time I'll buy boots with windows in them! Come here now and clean out these boots!"

Edward crept into the garage and took away the offending boots. He was in trouble again. It didn't seem to matter what he did, someone was always mad at him. Even if he was trying to do something helpful, it always seemed to go wrong.

"Edward! What are you *doing?*" cried his mother.

"I'm cleaning Dad's boots," said Edward placidly.

"On the living room *carpet?* Take those boots outside right now. And when you've finished with them, you can come right back and clear this mess up."

Edward picked up the boots and walked slowly outside. He felt sad and unloved. As he carried the boots, upside down, more mud fell out in little heaps behind him. Mrs. Teddington flopped down into a chair with a gasp. "What *are* we going to do with that bear?"

Mr. and Mrs. Teddington had an Emergency Meeting in the garage. "It's not that he's a bad little bear," said his mother. "He just doesn't ever *think* about what he's doing. He was very kind to you when you had a cold last month. He made that cocoa all by himself and brought it upstairs ever so carefully, without spilling a drop."

"That was so that he could spill the whole *mug* over my bed!" cried Mr. Teddington. "Never mind the cold. I nearly *drowned!*"

"Well, I think the problem is that he doesn't have an older bear to look up to and copy. I thought we could invite my friend Violet and her little boy Billy to stay with us."

"*Two* boys in the house?" Mr. Teddington shuddered. But then he remembered Billy handing out hymn books very quietly at Mrs. Teddington's sister's wedding, and he reluctantly agreed.

As soon as Billy arrived in the house, Mr. and Mrs. Teddington felt sure that they had done the right thing. Billy was clean and polite, but more importantly, he was *thoughtful*. After supper, Billy would say, "May I help with the washing up, Mrs. Teddington? I'll just go and put on my apron."

Billy washed Mr. Teddington's car and polished it so that you could see your face in it. *And* he saved the rinsing water for Mrs. Teddington's potted plants. "Waste not, want not," said Billy cheerfully.

"He's having a very good effect on Edward," whispered Mrs. Teddington to her husband. "He's such a *sensible* little bear. Although sometimes I think he is just a little bit *too* good. It's not quite natural somehow."

"Let's make the most of it," said her husband. "He's going home the day after tomorrow."

It had been a week without major accidents of any kind. Yes, Edward had somehow dropped his cereal into the toaster. But Billy had cleaned out the cereal and a lot of crumbs in the bottom. "A toaster can be dangerous, if you don't decrumb it regularly, Mr. Teddington," he said.

On Billy's last day, the whole family went for a picnic down by the river. Somehow Billy's presence made the whole thing rather quieter than picnics usually were. "Why don't you go and play with Billy, Edward?" said his parents, when they had all eaten.

"We're a little too near the riverbank for safety," said Billy. "One false step and a dangerous situation could occur."

"Oh, nonsense," cried Mr. Teddington. "Let's go and look for frogs." In no time at all, he and Edward were crawling along the bank. Billy stood a little further back. "Your knees are getting very muddy," he warned, "and grass stains are difficult to remove."

"What was that, Billy?" asked Mr. Teddington, looking over his shoulder for a moment. "Aaargh!" SPLASH! Edward's dad had fallen into the water!

At once, there was uproar. "He can't swim!" yelled Mrs. Teddington. "Somebody *do* something!"

"Dad!" cried Edward. "I'll save you!" And he plunged into the water.

"I shall stay safely away from the edge," said Billy calmly. "People are often drowned trying to save someone. It wouldn't be sensible to go closer."

But Mr. Teddington climbed out of the river with Edward in his arms. He had a broad smile on his face.

"In case you hadn't noticed, Billy," he said, "the water only came up to my knees. And before you say it, I *know* accidents can happen even in shallow water. But Edward is a very good swimmer and there are things that are more important than being sensible. I'm very proud of Edward."

Edward snuggled closer in his father's arms as his mother gave them both a big hug, not minding that she was getting very wet herself.

"There wasn't any need to worry," smiled Mr. Teddington.

"I wasn't really worried," said his wife. "Especially now I can see *exactly* where Edward gets his... Edwardness from!"

# A Bear at Bedtime

O ne teddy bear in a bed is cuddly,
Two teddy bears are better still.
And three teddy bears can't keep you as warm
As four teddy bears on your pillow will.

Five teddy bears will help you sleep,
And six teddy bears will hug you tight.
Seven teddy bears can be very friendly,
Eight teddy bears keep you safe at night.

But nine teddy bears in a bed?
There's only one problem that I can see:
Then there isn't any room for me!

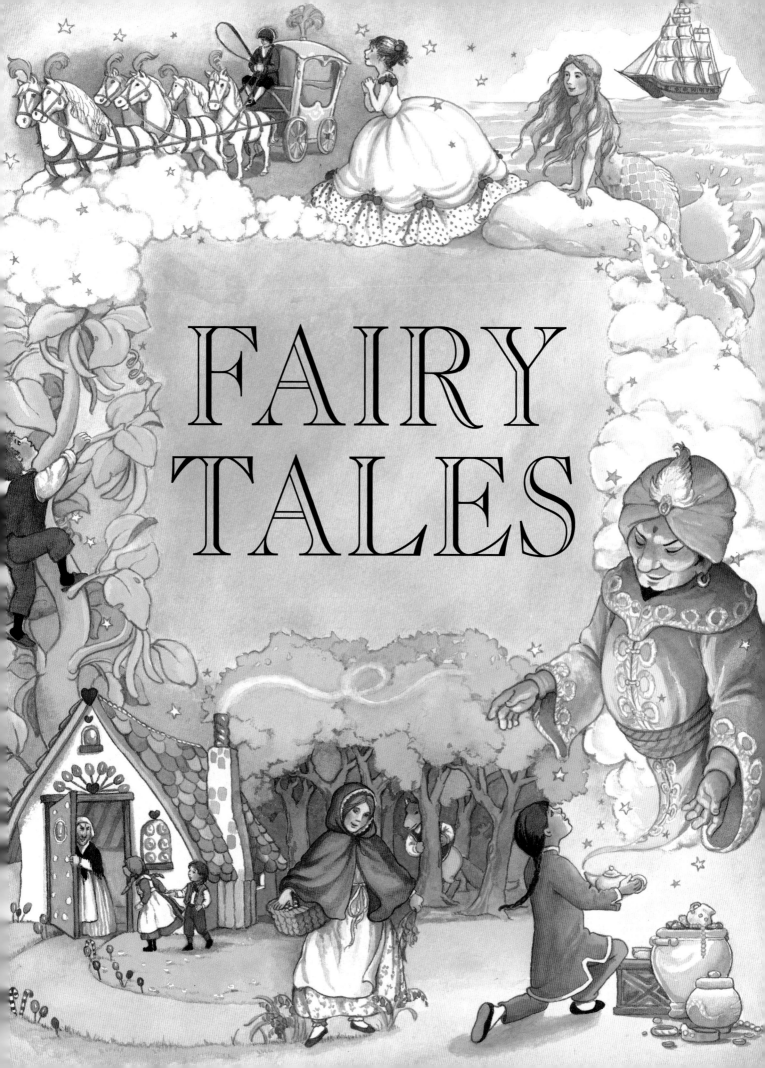

# FAIRY TALES

# Little Red Riding Hood

Once upon a time there was a little girl who lived on the edge of the woods. The clothes she liked best in all the world was a red cloak with a hood that her Granny had given to her. In fact, she liked it so much that she wore it nearly all the time. Because of this, everyone called her Little Red Riding Hood.

One morning, Little Red Riding Hood's mother sighed as she read a letter. "It's from Granny," she said, "and she's not feeling very well. But I just haven't time to go to see her today."

"I could go," said Little Red Riding Hood.

"Well," replied her mother, "I suppose you are quite a big girl now. I'll pack a basket of nice things for Granny and you can take it to her. But you must promise me not to wander off the path and not to talk to anyone on the way."

"Of course not," said Little Red Riding Hood.

So Little Red Riding Hood set off for her Granny's cottage on the other side of the woods. Her mother waved to her until she was out of sight among the trees.

It was a lovely day. The birds sang and little woodland animals peeped out to see Little Red Riding Hood go by. Soon she saw some lovely flowers growing beneath the trees.

"These would make a wonderful present for Granny," she said to herself, as she stopped to pick some. She forgot that her mother had told her not to wander off the path *at all*.

Just as Little Red Riding Hood had finished picking a big bunch of flowers, a wolf stepped out from behind a nearby tree.

"Good afternoon, my dear," he said. "What a charming bunch of flowers."

"I'm sorry," said Little Red Riding Hood firmly, "but I'm not allowed to talk to strangers. I'm on my way to see my Granny, and I mustn't be late." Then she walked quickly on down the path.

The wolf watched her go with a smile on his long, furry face. "Perhaps we shall meet again," he called. Then he ran off through the trees, following a secret shortcut that only wolves knew.

Half an hour later, Little Red Riding Hood arrived at her Granny's cottage. "That's strange," she thought. "Granny has left her door open." Little Red Riding Hood knocked on the open door and walked in.

It was quite dark inside the cottage and Little Red Riding Hood wondered whether Granny was asleep, so she tiptoed quietly over to the bed. Granny was wide awake and sitting up but she really didn't look very well at all. She was wearing a nightcap that didn't seem quite big enough.

"Why, Granny!" whispered Little Red Riding Hood. "What big ears you have!"

"The better to hear you with, my dear," said Granny in a strange voice. Little Red Riding Hood looked a little closer.

"Why, Granny!" she cried in surprise. "What big eyes you have!"

"The better to see you with, my dear," said Granny, pulling the covers up a little higher.

But Little Red Riding Hood had seen something very odd indeed. "Why, Granny!" she gasped. "What big teeth you have!"

"The better to eat you with, my dear!" shouted the wolf, leaping out of the bed and throwing off Granny's nightcap.

Little Red Riding Hood screamed at the top of her voice and ran to the door. Luckily, a woodman who was working nearby heard the scream and hurried in with his axe. The wolf was so frightened that he ran off into the trees.

"We won't be seeing him around here for a long while," said the woodman.

"Where's Granny?" cried Little Red Riding Hood. Just then there came a strange thumping sound from the wardrobe. The woodman opened the door, and out fell Granny!

"There's nothing like a good fright to cure a cold," she said cheerfully. " Now sit down, both of you, and I'll put the kettle on."

# The Little Mermaid

Long ago and far away, the King of the Mer-people ruled all the lands under the sea. He lived in a palace made of shells and precious pearls with his six beautiful mermaid daughters.

All day long the six mermaids played in the clear blue water, but they were not allowed to rise to the surface and look at the world where humans lived.

"The stories say that they have strange legs instead of tails," said the oldest Princess.

"Yes, and they live on land, not in the sea," said another.

"I wish I could see the lands they live in," sighed the youngest Princess.

"You are all much too young, all of you," said their grandmother. "But I will tell you strange tales of the world of human beings, if you are very good."

So every night, when the blue of the sea became dark and still, the Princesses listened to her stories. The youngest mermaid longed to be old enough to see for herself.

78

As the years passed, the Princesses grew up and were allowed to take their first look at the outside world. They came back with tales of great cities full of lights, and of strange wooden vessels that carried people across the sea. At last it was the turn of the youngest Princess. Trembling with excitement, she swam to the surface and gazed at the sunlit world. In the distance was one of the wooden ships that her sisters had described. The little mermaid swam up to it and saw a handsome young man laughing with his friends on the deck. Then the sky grew dark, and a great storm blew up. The ship was battered by the waves and driven upon rocks near the shore. The young man was thrown into the water, and the little mermaid knew that he would drown if she did not help him. Cradling him in her arms, she brought him safely to shore, leaving him on a sandy beach.

The little mermaid waited not far from the shore to see what would happen. Soon some young girls came along the beach and found the young man.

"It's the Prince!" they cried.

Slowly the Prince opened his eyes. "Where is the beautiful girl who saved me?" he asked. But no one could tell him.

The little mermaid swam sadly away, but no matter what she did, she could not forget the Prince, for she had fallen in love with him. At last, she could bear it no longer.

"I shall visit the sea witch and ask for her help," she said.

Deep in her cave, the sea witch cackled, "So you want to become human? It is quite painful, you know, to turn a mermaid's tail into legs, and I shall need some kind of payment."

"What can I give you?" asked the little mermaid.

"Your voice, my pretty," chuckled the witch.

"And shall I then truly be a human?"

"No, for that you must be loved by a human man," said the witch. "But if he chooses another, you will turn into sea foam before dawn."

So the little mermaid gave her lovely voice to the witch and became almost human. She joined the crowd of courtiers who were always coming and going in the Prince's palace. Before long, the Prince noticed the lovely girl and wished her to be always near him. The little mermaid had only one sorrow: without her voice, she could not tell the Prince who she was.

Although the Prince was fond of the lovely girl, his heart was full of the mystery woman who had saved him from drowning. He did not know that she was already by his side.

One day he told the little mermaid, "I am going to a far country where there lives a beautiful Princess. Perhaps I shall marry her." The little mermaid thought that her heart would break.

When the Prince met the lovely Princess, he was dazzled by her beauty. "You must be the girl who saved me," he cried and arrangements were made for the wedding to take place the next day.

The little mermaid knew that when the sun rose in the morning, she would turn into foam. That evening, she leaned over the rail of the ship and her tears dropped like pearls into the sea. Suddenly she saw her sisters swimming beneath the ship. "You can save yourself!" they cried. "You must kill the Prince with this knife and then you will be free!"

The little mermaid took the knife and crept to the Prince's cabin. But as she looked down at his sleeping face, she knew she loved him too much to harm him. Yet, when she threw herself into the sea, the little mermaid was not turned into foam. Instead she became a daughter of the air, helping those who are unhappy.

The next day, when the royal ship sailed, with the Prince and his bride on board, the little mermaid looked down on them and was able to smile at last.

# Cinderella

"Where's that girl? My hair needs brushing!"

"The fire's going out. Come here, lazybones!"

All day long, Cinderella's sisters yelled and scolded. From dawn to dusk she cleaned the house, fetched and carried, tended the fires and did the cooking, while her sisters lived a life of ease. Cinderella's clothes were dirty and torn. She had no fine jewels or pretty shoes, but still she was far more beautiful than her two ugly sisters. Of course, this made them dislike her even more.

One day there was great excitement in the town. A messenger from the palace went from door to door inviting all the young ladies from near and far to a ball to celebrate the Prince's birthday.

"It's time he was married," cried one ugly sister. "Perhaps he will choose a bride at the ball. Cinderella, alter my new ballgown, it has shrunk!"

"You may be right," said the other sister. "Cinderella, clean my dancing shoes!"

No one thought for a moment that the invitation included Cinderella.

On the night of the ball, Cinderella sat exhausted in front of the dying fire. In their hurry to get ready, her sisters had been even more unkind than usual. Cinderella stared into the glowing coals. "I wish that I could go to the ball," she sighed.

Suddenly the fire sparkled to life and a smiling old woman stood in the kitchen.

"I am your fairy godmother, Cinderella," she said. "And you *shall* go to the ball."

The fairy asked Cinderella to bring her a pumpkin. With a wave of her wand, she turned it into a beautiful golden coach with four handsome footmen.

"Now bring me six mice," she cried. In a moment, the fairy turned the mice into six beautiful horses to pull the coach. "Now you are ready for the ball, my dear," she smiled.

Cinderella looked down at her ragged clothes. "I can't go to the palace like this," she whispered.

The fairy laughed and waved her wand for a third time. In a second, Cinderella was clothed in the most beautiful satin dress she had ever seen. Rosebuds nestled in her silky hair and on her feet were dainty glass slippers. "How can I ever thank you?" she asked.

"Just enjoy yourself!" replied the fairy. "But remember, the magic only lasts until midnight. Before the clock strikes, you must hurry home."

When Cinderella arrived at the ball in her golden coach, everyone in the palace wondered who the beautiful stranger could be. The Prince himself led her to the ballroom and would let no one else dance with her all evening. Floating around the room in the Prince's arms, Cinderella almost cried with happiness. She forgot everything but the handsome young man who smiled down at her.

But as she whirled around the floor, Cinderella suddenly heard the great clock on the tower outside begin to strike. It was midnight!

"I'm sorry," whispered Cinderella and she ran from the ballroom. She was just in time. As she fled across the square, her clothes began to turn to rags. By the time the bewildered Prince reached the steps outside the palace, she had disappeared from sight. All that was left was a single glass slipper, shining in the moonlight.

At home next day, Cinderella's sisters could talk of nothing but the girl who had stolen the Prince's heart.

"No one else danced with him *at all*," they complained. "And they say that he is looking everywhere for her."

The sisters did not know about the glass slipper, but the next day, a royal messenger arrived with an escort of soldiers. "The Prince has commanded that every girl in the kingdom must try on this slipper," he said. "And the Prince has vowed to marry the one whom it fits."

"Let me try!" cried the first ugly sister. She tried with all her might to squeeze her fat foot into the slipper, but it was no use.

"My turn I think, my dear," said the second ugly sister with a sneer. But her thin foot was much too long for the tiny slipper.

"Is there anyone else in the house?" asked the royal messenger.

"Only a maid," laughed the sisters. "The slipper will *never* fit *her*." But the messenger was firm: every girl must try it on.

So Cinderella was brought from the kitchen. Blushing, she put on the dainty slipper, just as the Prince himself entered the house to see how the search was proceeding.

"It was *you*!" he cried, looking down at Cinderella's lovely face. "Please be my bride and we shall never be parted again."

It seemed as though the whole world lined the streets to cheer when Cinderella married her Prince. Even the ugly sisters were happy. They had received invitations to the grand ball after the wedding, and they had heard that many visiting Princes would certainly be there....

# Snow White and the Seven Dwarfs

O ne winter's day, a Queen sat sewing by a castle window. As she sewed, she pricked her finger and three drops of blood fell on the snow by the black window frame.

"I wish that my daughter could have skin as white as snow, lips as red as blood and hair as black as this window frame," sighed the Queen.

Very soon afterward, the Queen gave birth to a beautiful daughter, just as she had described. She named her Snow White.

Sadly, the Queen died soon after, leaving her baby to be brought up by Snow White's father, the King.

Now the King had loved his wife very much, but after some years he grew lonely and decided to marry again. His bride was a very beautiful woman but her heart was cold. Every day she looked into a magic mirror and asked:

*"Mirror, mirror, on the wall,*
*Who is the fairest of them all?"*

And the mirror would reply:

*"Many are lovely beyond compare,*
*But you, O Queen, are fairest of the fair."*

The new Queen did not like children and made sure that she never saw Snow White. She did not know that each day the young princess grew more lovely. Finally the day came when the mirror gave a new reply:

*"You, O Queen, are lovely beyond compare,*
*But Snow White is the fairest of the fair."*

The Queen became enraged. She summoned a huntsman and ordered him to take Snow White into the forest and kill her.

"Bring me back her heart," hissed the evil Queen, "so that I can be sure she is dead."

The huntsman was not a cruel man but he feared for his life, so he led Snow White into the thickest part of the forest. But when he looked down at her lovely face, he could not kill her. Instead he left her there and took back an animal's heart to deceive the Queen.

Alone in the forest as night began to fall, Snow White was terrified. She stumbled through the trees, not knowing which way to go. At last she saw a little house standing in a clearing. Worn out with fear and hunger, she crept inside and fell asleep on the first of the seven little beds that lined the wall.

A few hours later, Snow White awoke to find seven little men looking down at her. At first she was frightened, but after she had told them her tale, the seven dwarfs spoke kindly to her.

"You poor child," said one. "Of course you can stay with us. But you must be very careful, for the wicked Queen may find out that you are still alive."

So Snow White looked after the dwarfs and kept their little house clean. She was very happy, although she was left alone when the dwarfs went off to work each morning.

One day an old woman knocked on the door. "Pretty things for a pretty girl!" she called. Snow White opened the door eagerly. She was glad to have a visitor, and could not tell that the old woman was really the wicked Queen in disguise. "Let me tie this pretty ribbon around your neck," smiled the old woman.

To her horror, Snow White felt the ribbon being pulled tighter and tighter, until she fell down as though she were dead.

That night the dwarfs found their friend lying where she had fallen. Tenderly, they nursed her back to life, but they spoke to her sternly.

"You must *never* open the door to *anyone* again," they said. "Next time you may not be so lucky."

Time passed and all was well. But after a few months, an old woman with a basket of apples came to the door of the little house. "I won't come in, my dear," she said. "Let me pass you this special apple through the window. You've never tasted anything so sweet!"

Poor Snow White took just one bite of the apple. It was poisoned! When the dwarfs came home, all their loving care could not revive her.

"This is the Queen's work," they said angrily. The dwarfs could not bear to bury Snow White, so they put her in a glass coffin in a clearing of the forest and kept watch beside her.

One day a Prince came riding by. The moment he saw Snow White, he fell in love with her. "Though she can never be my bride," he said to the dwarfs, "let me take her back to my palace, to rest in the surroundings she deserves."

Reluctantly, the dwarfs agreed, and the Prince ordered his men to pick up the coffin. But as they did so, the piece of apple that had caught in Snow White's throat was dislodged. To everyone's amazement, she stretched her arms and sat up, and the first person she set eyes on was the handsome young Prince, smiling down at her.

Of course, Snow White married her Prince and all the dwarfs danced at her wedding. As for the evil Queen, she was so furious that she flew away in a tantrum and was never seen there again.

# Thumbelina

Once there was a woman who longed to have a little girl of her own. She went to a wise woman and asked for her help.

"Take this seed," said the old woman kindly, "and plant it in a pot. You will see your wish come true."

The woman did as she was told. She watered the seed in its pot and soon two leaves pushed their way through the soil. In a few days, a flower bud could be seen, which opened to reveal a beautiful yellow flower. There, right in the middle of the flower, was a little girl no bigger than the woman's thumb.

"I will call her Thumbelina," cried the delighted woman joyfully.

Little Thumbelina was looked after very well. Her mother made her tiny little clothes and a bed from a walnut shell.

But one day, as Thumbelina sat on the table singing to herself, an old mother toad hopped in through the window and carried Thumbelina away.

"You are so beautiful," croaked the toad to the frightened little girl. "You shall be married to my son." And she left Thumbelina on a lily pad in the middle of the river.

Thumbelina began to cry. She did not want to be married to an ugly toad and live in the mud on the riverbank. Some little fish who were swimming past saw her tears and decided to help her. They nibbled through the stalk of the lily pad so that it floated off down the river.

Thumbelina cheered up as she drifted along. There were flowers on the bank and pretty butterflies fluttered around her head. But the little girl's adventures were not over. A huge black beetle flew down and carried her off to the tall tree where his family lived.

"What ever is *that*?" jeered the other beetles. "It's only got two legs. How very ugly!" So the beetle let Thumbelina go.

All summer long, Thumbelina was happy once more. She made friends with the birds and butterflies and ate berries and seeds. At night she slept in an empty bird's nest. But when summer came to an end, her friends disappeared and food became scarce. She was too cold to sleep at night.

One day, shivering and hungry, Thumbelina met a fieldmouse coming out of her nest. "You can stay with me for a little while," said the mouse.

Thumbelina liked the snug little nest very much, but it was very small. "You must meet my friend the mole," said the mouse. "He is looking for a wife and he has a great big home underground."

So Thumbelina went to see the mole's home. It was dark and cold as the mole led her through the narrow passages. "Be careful here," said the mole. "Something has died in my tunnel."

92

Thumbelina bent down and felt the body of a swallow. It was very cold but its heart was still beating! "I will look after you and make you well," whispered Thumbelina. She brought the bird food and covered him with leaves to keep him warm. Before long, he was ready to fly away. Thumbelina waved until she could no longer see him.

When the spring sunshine warmed the earth once more, Thumbelina sat looking sadly at the blue sky. It was time for her to marry the mole, but she dreaded living underground and never seeing sunshine or the pretty spring flowers. Suddenly she saw a bird high above. It was the swallow that she had saved!

"Climb on to my back," said the swallow, "and I will take you to a faraway land where it is always warm and the flowers never die."

Thumbelina clung to the swallow's feathers as he flew across land and sea. At last the swallow landed in a flowery meadow. As Thumbelina looked around her, she was amazed to see that every flower had a little person sitting in it – tiny people, just like her! One little man came forward, smiling.

"I am the King of the flower people," he said. "Welcome to our land. We will call you Maia."

Thumbelina was overjoyed to have found so many friends. She grew to love the little King who had greeted her, and lived happily ever after among the flower people as their Queen.

# Rumpelstiltskin

Once upon a time there was a very silly man who had a beautiful daughter. The King heard tell of the lovely girl and summoned her father to the palace. Overcome by such grand surroundings, the man talked all kinds of nonsense. "Not only is my daughter beautiful," he boasted to the King, "but she can also spin straw into gold."

The King smiled, for he loved money more than anything. "Bring her to the palace," he cried, "and if she can do as you say, I will marry her!"

So the poor girl was brought to the palace and shut into a tiny room with nothing but a pile of straw and a spinning wheel.

"You have until morning to spin that straw into gold," said the King. "But if you fail, you must die."

As the door clanged shut behind her, the girl burst into tears. She hadn't the faintest idea of how to begin spinning straw into gold.

Suddenly, with a puff of smoke, a strange little man appeared before her. "Why all these tears, pretty one?" he asked.

Sobbing, the girl explained her dilemma.

"But that's easily solved," laughed the strange little man. "You give me... let's see... your gold ring... and I'll spin this straw into gold."

The poor girl was only too glad to make the exchange. Long before morning, the little man had done as he had promised, then disappeared as quickly as he had come, leaving the girl alone.

The King was delighted when he saw the golden thread, and at once he wanted more. "We must be sure that this was not a trick," he said. "Tonight you shall have even more straw to spin."

That night the strange little man appeared again. He chuckled when he saw the huge pile of straw. "Child's play!" he cried. "But I shall need payment, pretty one. Your glass beads, perhaps?"

Eagerly, the girl handed over her necklace. The little man sat down next to her immediately and began to spin. By morning, he had disappeared, leaving behind several skeins of golden thread.

"This is splendid!" said the King when he saw it. "You will not object, I am sure, to one more test? If you pass again, you shall certainly become my Queen."

This time there was a whole room full of straw for the girl to spin. When she was left by herself, she cried so bitterly that she did not see the little man appear.

"What's the matter, pretty one?" he asked. "Surely you know that I will help you?"

"But I have nothing left to give you," sobbed the unhappy girl.

"No matter," said the little man. "When you are Queen, you shall give me your first-born child. That will be payment enough."

This seemed so unlikely to happen that the girl agreed at once and the little man sat down to spin. When the King opened the door the next morning, the girl sat amid a hundred skeins of thread, lit by their golden glow. The King had never seen anything so beautiful, and he ordered that their wedding should take place at once.

A year passed. The new Queen was happier than she could ever have believed, especially when she gave birth to a lovely baby daughter. But one night, as she got ready for bed, she was startled to see the strange little man standing beside the baby's cradle.

"It's time for you to carry out your promise, pretty one," he said.

The young Queen was terrified. "I will give you anything else you want," she cried. "Take my jewels! Take my crown!"

But the little man just laughed. "I am not a cruel man," he said. "If you can guess my name before three nights have passed, you will never see me again."

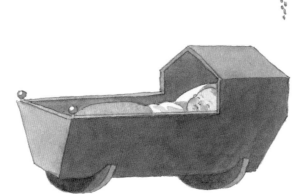

On the next two nights, the Queen guessed every name she could think of. She asked her soldiers to ride through the kingdom collecting the strangest names they could find. But at every name the little man just chuckled and shook his head.

On the third day a soldier came to the Queen and told her a strange story. "As I was riding through the forest," he said, "I saw an odd little man dancing around a fire, singing:

*'The Queen will never win my game,*
*For Rumpelstiltskin is my name!'*"

That night the little man appeared once more before the Queen.

"Is your name... Hurly Burly?" she asked.
"No!" cried the little man.
"Then is it... Humpelby Bumpelby?"
"No! No!"
"Then perhaps it is... Rumpelstiltskin?"
At that the little man turned red with fury. He stamped his feet so hard that he fell right through the floor.

The young Queen lived happily ever after and never saw the strange little man again.

# Hansel and Gretel

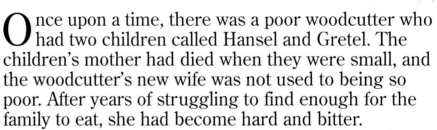

Once upon a time, there was a poor woodcutter who had two children called Hansel and Gretel. The children's mother had died when they were small, and the woodcutter's new wife was not used to being so poor. After years of struggling to find enough for the family to eat, she had become hard and bitter.

One evening, as the two hungry children tried to get to sleep, they heard their father and stepmother talking in the next room.

"We cannot afford to feed ourselves *and* the children," said the woman. "At this rate, we shall *all* starve. Tomorrow, we must take the children into the forest and leave them there."

The woodcutter protested, but he could not bear to lose his wife, and in the end he agreed.

The children were very frightened, but Hansel comforted his sister. "Don't worry," he said. "I'll slip out and find some white stones. If I drop them along the path, we'll be able to find our way home."

The next day, Hansel did just as he had said. The woodcutter and his wife left the children in the forest, promising to return, but they returned home instead. Still, Hansel and Gretel were able to find their way in the moonlight, following the white pebbles until they saw their cottage ahead.

The woodcutter was overjoyed to see them, but his wife set her mouth in a hard line and looked away.

A week later, she persuaded her husband that they must follow their plan again. This time, she locked the children in their room so that Hansel could not go out and gather pebbles.

"I'll drop crumbs from a piece of dry bread kept from breakfast," he told Gretel. "We can follow them, just as we did the pebbles."

Once again, the woodcutter and his wife left the children and set off for home.

But when Hansel and Gretel tried to follow the trail of breadcrumbs, they found that the birds had eaten them all! Hungry and afraid, they stumbled through the forest, not knowing which way to turn.

"Look!" cried Gretel suddenly, pointing through the trees. There was a strange little house with a roof and walls of gingerbread and windows of sugar. The hungry children ran toward it. "This is delicious!" cried Hansel, with his mouth full, but a voice interrupted him.

"Who's that eating my house?" it cackled, and the two children jumped with fright. An old woman had come out of the house and was watching them with beady eyes. She was a witch who liked to eat little children, so at first she pretended to be kind.

"Come inside and I will give you some good bread and soup," she said. When Hansel and Gretel had eaten their fill, she tucked them up in bed.

But the next morning, the witch locked Hansel in a shed and forced Gretel to work night and day cooking food for him. "Soon he'll be fat enough for me to eat," chuckled the witch, rubbing her hands.

Every day the witch asked Hansel to poke his finger out between the bars to see if he was fat enough yet. But clever Hansel poked out a chicken bone instead. "Still *much* too scrawny," whined the witch.

At last the day came when the witch could wait no longer. She ordered Gretel to stoke up the fire under the oven. "Just poke your head in and see if it is hot enough yet, my dear," she said. But Gretel was afraid that the witch would push her in, so she pretended not to understand. Angrily, the old woman pushed her aside and peered in herself. In a flash, the little girl gave the witch a big push.

Slamming the oven door shut, Gretel ran to the shed to set her brother free.

Hansel and Gretel laughed with happiness as they ran from the witch's house, but they still did not know how to find their way home. Then a bird flying high above called to them. "I ate your breadcrumbs before," it chirped. "I will lead you home."

So Hansel and Gretel followed the bird and came at last to the woodcutter's cottage. Their father wept with joy to see them. His wife had gone back to her own family, and not a day had passed since then that he had not searched in vain for his children.

"We have one more surprise," smiled Hansel and Gretel, emptying their pockets. "We found lots of gold and silver coins in the witch's house. We shall never be poor again!"

And so, Hansel and Gretel and their father lived together happily ever after in the little cottage.

# Rapunzel

A long time ago there lived a woman who longed above everything to have a baby of her own. She wanted this so much that she became ill and her husband grew worried about her.

One day the woman looked out of her bedroom window and saw some lettuce growing in the garden next door. "I feel as though I shall die if I don't eat some of that lettuce," she said to her husband. "Please go and get some for me."

The man was so anxious to do anything for his wife that he agreed. This was very brave of him, for it was well known that a witch lived in the house next door.

Late that night the man crept over the wall between the two gardens and made his way to the vegetable garden. He had just picked a fine head of lettuce, when he heard a soft sound behind him.

"So," hissed a voice. "You think that you can steal anything of mine you like."

It was the witch, silvery in the moonlight. The man was so shaken with fear that he could hardly stand. "Please let me go," he begged. "I'll do anything."

"Very well," said the witch. "Bring me your baby daughter on the day that she is born."

The man agreed at once, for he had given up hope of having a child of his own.

But several months later, his wife did give birth to a baby girl and, true to his promise, the man took her straight to the witch.

The man and his wife never saw the child again, but the witch took very good care of her. She called the little girl Rapunzel.

As she grew older, Rapunzel became very beautiful, and the witch began to worry that other people would notice her beauty, so she took the girl to a tall tower in a forest. There was no door in the tower and no stairs – just a room at the top with one small window.

In this room, Rapunzel sat all day.

When the witch wanted to visit Rapunzel, she would stand at the bottom of the tower and call, "Rapunzel, Rapunzel, let down your hair." The girl would lower her thick plait of hair from the window, and the witch would climb up it.

One day, when the witch visited Rapunzel, a Prince happened to be riding through the forest. He had heard sweet singing coming from the tower and wondered who lived there. Hidden among the trees, he watched what happened and waited until the witch was gone. Then he went to the bottom of the tower and called softly, "Rapunzel, Rapunzel, let down your hair."

Rapunzel thought it was strange that the witch should come back so soon, but she did as she was asked. She was astonished to see the young man climbing into the room. The Prince was dazzled by the beautiful girl and spoke to her gently, promising that he would visit again. Rapunzel found that she liked the Prince very much. Very soon, she fell deeply in love with him.

One day, when the witch came to see Rapunzel, the girl said without thinking, "Why is it that you feel so much heavier climbing up my hair than the Prince does?"

The witch screamed with fury. "You have deceived me!" she cried. With a huge pair of scissors she snipped off Rapunzel's hair, and banished her to a faraway desert. Then she lay in wait for the Prince, determined to have her revenge.

When the Prince stood at the foot of the tower, he called out as usual, "Rapunzel, Rapunzel, let down your hair." The witch lowered Rapunzel's cut hair from the window. It was not until he was nearly at thc top that the Prince saw the witch's face laughing cruelly down at him. With a cry of horror, he fell from the tower into the thorns and brambles below.

The Prince was not killed, but his eyes were blinded by the thorns. For years he wandered in search of Rapunzel, visiting many lands. At last, one day he came to the desert and heard the sweet singing that he had feared he would never hear again.

"Rapunzel!" he cried, running toward her. As he clasped Rapunzel in his arms, her tears of joy touched his eyes and his sight returned.

Hand in hand, Rapunzel and her Prince travelled to his kingdom. Great rejoicing was heard throughout the land when the people found that their Prince was alive and had found so beautiful a bride.

# Jack and the Beanstalk

"It's no good," said Jack's mother one day. "We shall have to sell our cow. We have no money left and you are such a lazy, silly boy, Jack, that you will never find work."

So Jack set off to market with the cow, but on the way he met a stranger. "Why walk all the way to market?" asked the man. "I will take the cow off your hands right away and I'll give you these magic beans in return. I think you'll agree, that's a bargain!"

Jack was delighted to have a handful of magic beans and he handed over the cow immediately.

But Jack's mother was *furious*. "You are a stupid, idle boy!" she cried, "and you will go straight to bed without any supper!" Then she threw the beans out of the window.

The next morning, when Jack woke up, he thought that the room seemed very dark. He looked out of his window and was astonished to see that an enormous bean plant had grown beside the house. Its top disappeared into the clouds.

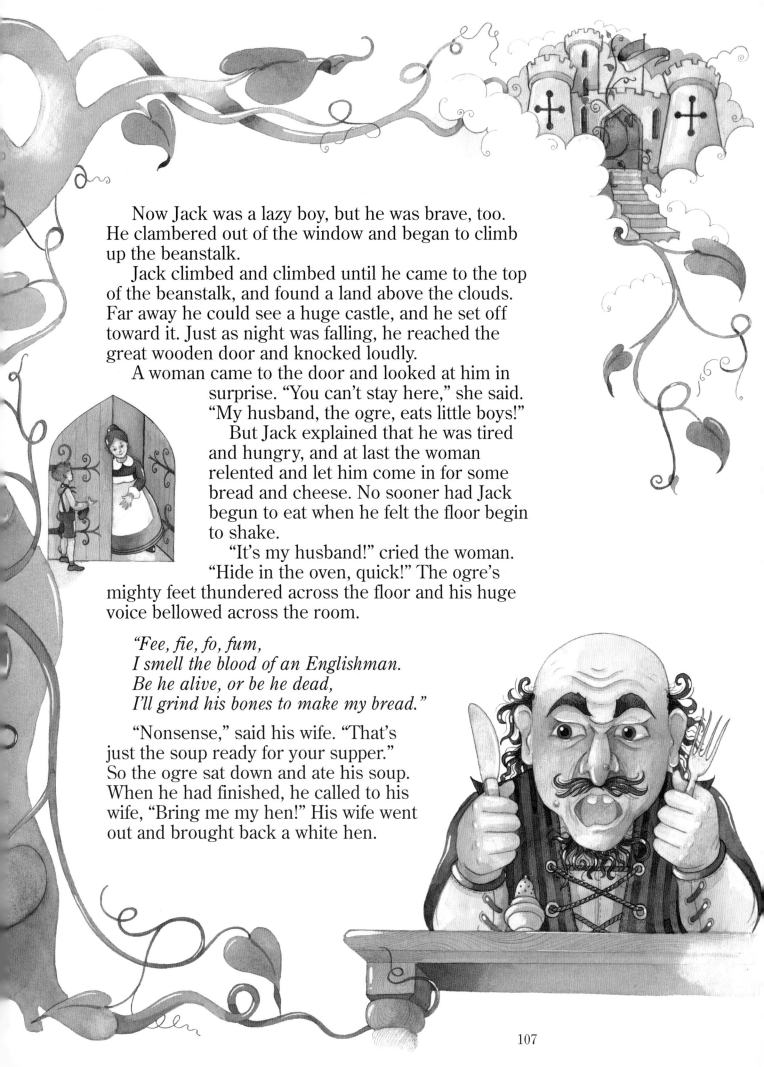

Now Jack was a lazy boy, but he was brave, too. He clambered out of the window and began to climb up the beanstalk.

Jack climbed and climbed until he came to the top of the beanstalk, and found a land above the clouds. Far away he could see a huge castle, and he set off toward it. Just as night was falling, he reached the great wooden door and knocked loudly.

A woman came to the door and looked at him in surprise. "You can't stay here," she said. "My husband, the ogre, eats little boys!"

But Jack explained that he was tired and hungry, and at last the woman relented and let him come in for some bread and cheese. No sooner had Jack begun to eat when he felt the floor begin to shake.

"It's my husband!" cried the woman. "Hide in the oven, quick!" The ogre's mighty feet thundered across the floor and his huge voice bellowed across the room.

*"Fee, fie, fo, fum,*
*I smell the blood of an Englishman.*
*Be he alive, or be he dead,*
*I'll grind his bones to make my bread."*

"Nonsense," said his wife. "That's just the soup ready for your supper." So the ogre sat down and ate his soup. When he had finished, he called to his wife, "Bring me my hen!" His wife went out and brought back a white hen.

The ogre took the hen and shouted, "Lay!" To Jack's amazement, as he peeped out of the oven door, the hen laid a golden egg! Again and again the ogre ordered the hen to lay, until there were twelve golden eggs on the table. Then the ogre fell asleep and began to snore.

When he heard the ogre snoring, Jack jumped out of the oven, picked up the magic hen, and ran away as fast as his legs would carry him. He scrambled down the beanstalk and stood, breathless, in front of his mother.

"Why Jack!" she cried. "That is the hen that the wicked ogre stole from your poor father. Now our troubles are over!"

But although Jack and his mother became quite wealthy, the boy still had a spirit of adventure. One day he climbed the beanstalk again and made his way to the ogre's castle. Once again he hid, and heard the ogre's great voice:

*"Fee, fie, fo, fum,*
*I smell the blood of an Englishman.*
*Be he alive, or be he dead,*
*I'll grind his bones to make my bread."*

The ogre's wife brought him his supper and Jack was safe. After supper, the ogre called for his money bags. As Jack watched, he counted out bags and bags of gold coins.

"As soon as he falls asleep, I will take those money bags," said Jack to himself. And so he did. Again, Jack's mother was delighted. "This money belonged to your father, too," she said.

Jack decided to climb the beanstalk one more time. Everything happened just as before, but this time after supper the ogre called for his golden harp. When the ogre's wife brought the harp to the table, the ogre commanded, "Play!" At once the harp began to play the sweetest music Jack had ever heard.

No sooner had the ogre fallen asleep than Jack seized the harp and ran out of the door. But the harp called out, "Master! Master!" and the ogre awoke. With thundering footsteps, he chased after the boy. Jack ran as fast as he could to the top of the beanstalk but all the time he could hear the ogre getting nearer and nearer. He scrambled down as quickly as he could, but the ogre followed him. When he was nearly at the bottom, Jack called out, "Mother, mother, bring the axe!"

When he reached the ground, Jack took the axe and with one great blow he cut through the huge beanstalk. The ogre came tumbling down to his death.

As for Jack and his mother, they lived happily ever after.

# The Gingerbread Man

Once upon a time, a little old man and a little old woman lived together in a cottage in the country. One day, the little old woman made some gingerbread. When she had rolled out the dough and cut out all the rounds she wanted, she still had some dough left over.

"I will make a little gingerbread man," she said to herself, "as a surprise for my husband."

So she cut out the shape of a gingerbread man. She gave him three buttons and two eyes made of raisins and a smiley mouth made from a cherry. Then she put him in the oven with the other cookies.

Soon the delicious smell of baking cookies filled the kitchen. But when the little old woman went to take them out of the oven, she thought she heard a faint voice inside. She opened the oven door and almost fell over with surprise. The little gingerbread man jumped up from the tray and ran toward the kitchen door, as fast as his legs would carry him!

"Come back!" shouted the little old woman, running after him.

"Come back!" shouted the little old man, who was working in the garden.

They both ran after the gingerbread man. But the bold gingerbread man called over his shoulder.

"Run, run, as fast as you can! You won't catch me, I'm the gingerbread man!"

The gingerbread man ran down the garden path and out on to the road.

As he ran, he passed a cow in a field.

"Stop!" mooed the cow. "You look much nicer to eat than this grass." And she too ran after the little gingerbread man.

But the gingerbread man didn't stop for a second. "A little old woman and a little old man couldn't catch me, and neither will you! Run, run, as fast as you can! You won't catch me, I'm the gingerbread man!" he called out.

In the next field, he passed a horse. "Stop!" neighed the horse. "You look much nicer to eat than this hay."

But the gingerbread man kept running. "A little old woman and a little old man and a cow couldn't catch me, and neither will you! Run, run, as fast as you can! You won't catch me, I'm the gingerbread man!" he shouted.

A rooster sitting on a gate saw the gingerbread man. "Stop!" he cock-a-doodle-dooed. "You look much nicer to eat than this grain." And he flapped after the gingerbread man. But the naughty little figure just laughed. "A little old woman and a little old man and a cow and a horse couldn't catch me," he called, "and neither will you! Run, run, as fast as you can! You won't catch me, I'm the gingerbread man!"

Just then the gingerbread man passed a pig in a yard. "Stop!" grunted the pig. "You look much nicer to eat than this slop."

The gingerbread man ran even faster. "A little old woman and a little old man and a cow and a horse and a rooster couldn't catch me," he called, "and neither will you! Run, run, as fast as you can! You won't catch me, I'm the gingerbread man!"

But at the end of the next field, the little gingerbread man came to a wide river, and there he had to stop. For although gingerbread men are very good at running, they don't know how to swim at all.

"Can I help you?" asked a quiet voice nearby. It was a big red fox. "Perhaps you need some assistance in crossing the river? Pray allow me to help. Just jump on my back and I will carry you across."

The gingerbread man gratefully did as the fox said, for his pursuers were coming closer and closer. Without hesitating, the fox swam into the fast-flowing river.

But soon the fox spoke again. "The water is getting deeper. Climb on to my head and you will stay dry." And the gingerbread man did so.

"The water is even deeper here," said the fox soon. "Climb on to my nose and you will stay dry."

No sooner had the gingerbread man climbed on to the fox's head when the fox smiled a wide smile. He threw up his head and the gingerbread man flew up into the air. Then down he fell, right into the fox's open mouth.

Pretty soon, the little old woman and the little old man and the cow and the horse and the rooster came puffing up to the bank of the river. The gingerbread man was nowhere to be seen, But in the middle of the river, a duck pecked at a few last crumbs floating on the water.

# Sleeping Beauty

Long ago there lived a King and Queen who ruled over a great kingdom. When their first child was born, there was great rejoicing and they held a big party to celebrate her birth. The proud parents made sure to invite all the most important people in the kingdom, including twelve fairies who lived in the most distant parts of the land.

The party was a great success. All the guests brought expensive presents for the baby Princess, but the most valuable gifts of all came frolll the twelve fairies. One by one they stood over her cradle and smiled down at her.

"For my gift, I will give her beauty," said the first fairy, and everyone applauded.

"For my gift, I will give her a loving nature," said the second fairy, to loud cheers. And so it went on, as eleven of the fairies gave their gifts, until everyone felt that the Princess was going to be the loveliest, luckiest girl in the world.

Suddenly, before the twelfth fairy could speak, a rush of cold air blew through the room as the great doors were flung open. There on the doorstep stood a very old woman. It was some seconds before anyone recognized her. She was the thirteenth fairy, who lived among the highest mountains of the kingdom. Nothing had been heard of her for so many years that the King and Queen had completely forgotten to invite her.

The thirteenth fairy walked toward the cradle. "How lucky," she cackled, "that I was able to get here in time to give my gift to the Princess. Now you'll all be sorry that you left me out. The Princess will be happy and healthy until the day that she is eighteen years old. On that day she will prick her finger on a spindle and die."

With that the thirteenth fairy swept out of the room, leaving behind a stunned silence. Softly, the twelfth fairy stepped forward.

"I cannot undo my sister's words," she said, "but I can make them easier to bear. The Princess will still prick her finger, but instead of dying, she will fall asleep for one hundred years, until she is woken by her true love's kiss."

As the Princess grew up, the King and Queen took great care of her. While she was still a baby, they had all the spindles in the kingdom collected together and burned. As everyone had wished, the Princess grew up to be kind and happy and beautiful.

On the morning of her eighteenth birthday, the Princess awoke early and walked in the courtyard of the palace. She was looking forward to the celebrations that would be held later in the day. Suddenly she noticed a little door in a tower that she had never seen before. Overcome with curiosity, she opened the door and climbed the winding staircase inside.

At the top of the steps was another door. The Princess opened it and found a little room in which an old woman sat spinning.

Of course, the Princess had never seen a spinning wheel and a spindle. She stepped forward and asked the old woman what she was doing.

"Why, I'm spinning," came the reply. "Would you like to try, my dear? Come closer." And as she spoke, the old woman handed the lovely girl the spindle. As the Princess took it, she pricked her finger and fell at once into a deep, deep sleep.

The thirteenth fairy's words had come true. Not only did the Princess sleep in the little tower, but the whole castle stopped just at that moment. The King and Queen slept in the royal apartments. The cook slept in the kitchen. The guards slept at the gate. Even the hunting dogs slept in the great hall. Nothing stirred in the silent castle but the flags on the turrets fluttering gently in the breeze.

Years passed, and a great hedge of brambles and briars grew up around the palace. One day a young Prince happened to be riding by. He saw a tower above the brambles and asked his servant what it was.

"Well, there's an old legend," replied the page. "Some people say that a beautiful Princess lies asleep inside. But no one has been able to reach the palace for one hundred years."

The Prince was interested by the story. He took out his sword and hacked his way through the thorny hedge, on which hundreds of flowers bloomed. When he came to the palace itself, he was astonished to find the whole place asleep, just as at the moment when the Princess pricked her finger.

At last the Prince came to the tower where the Princess lay. He looked down at the lovely girl and at once fell in love with her, although he feared she was dead. He could not resist bending down to kiss her.

The Prince's kiss broke the thirteenth fairy's spell. As the Princess awoke, the whole palace came back to life. But in the little tower room, the Princess had eyes only for the young man leaning over her.

So the Princess's birthday was a day of great celebration. And very soon there was cause for an even bigger party, when the Princess married her Prince. But you can be sure that this time, the King and Queen were very careful indeed about the guest list.

# The Emperor's New Clothes

O nce upon a time, there was an Emperor who was very vain. Of course, all his life his courtiers had been telling him how wonderful he was. It was not surprising that he had begun to believe it himself. The more sure the Emperor became that he was the most intelligent, most handsome man in the kingdom, the less he liked to hear any criticism at all.

One day, the Emperor decided that he would like a new suit of clothes. "Something befitting a man in my position," he said. "Something grander than anything ever worn before." And because he wanted this suit to be so special, the Emperor did not believe that any of his usual tailors were good enough to make it.

It so happened that in the court at this time there were two wicked men who were looking for a chance to become rich. They presented themselves to the Emperor and announced that they could make him a suit unlike anything that had ever been made before.

"It is made of a new material," said one, "so fine that only the truly intelligent can see it. Ordinary people are too stupid to appreciate it at all."

This sounded like just the thing to the Emperor, and he asked them to set to work at once. Thus the performance began. The two tailors were given a room in the palace in which to work, and every day they asked for more money to buy the thread and cloth they needed. Of course, they did not buy anything at all, but stored up the money for themselves.

The Emperor was measured for his new suit. "This is not the way I have been measured before," he said doubtfully.

"But, Your Highness," replied the two men, "this new material requires improved methods, as a man of your intelligence will appreciate."

"Of course, of course," said the Emperor hastily.

At last the day came for the first fitting of the suit. The two greedy men pretended to hold something up before the Emperor.

"Isn't it beautiful?" they gushed. "We are particularly pleased with the buttonholes. A real triumph, I'm sure you agree." The Emperor hesitated. He could see nothing at all. So he asked his High Steward's opinion.

The High Steward was very frightened of appearing stupid before his Emperor, although he could see nothing at all either. "It is quite beyond words," he said slowly. "I can't find expressions to do it justice, Your Highness."

At that, the Emperor was even more uneasy. "I can't possibly appear more stupid than my High Steward," he said to himself. Out loud he said, "Well, this is quite extraordinary. I can truthfully say that I have never seen anything like it."

Then the tailors pretended to try the suit on the Emperor. "Do you feel that the sleeves should be a *little* longer, Your Highness?" they asked.

"Perhaps just a trifle," said the Emperor, "and I wonder if the collar needs a little adjustment." He found it easier as time went on to think of things to say about a suit of clothes that he could not see at all.

Several more fittings took place before the suit was finally declared to be finished. The tailors dressed the Emperor with care. He was to appear that day in a Grand Parade through the city.

When they had finished, the two wicked men stood back and admired the Emperor. "Stunning!" they cried. "Quite, quite remarkable. We only wish that we could stay for the parade but, alas, we must be on our way this very morning."

Of course, the Emperor rewarded the two men handsomely and even gave them a dignified royal wave as they rode quite hastily away.

At last, with a fanfare of trumpets and a roll of drums, the Emperor led the parade from the palace. The whole population of the city was lining the streets.

As the Emperor appeared, there was a small silence. But no one there wanted to appear more stupid than his friends.

"I've never seen anything like it," cried one man.

"Unique," said his wife. Soon everyone was cheering the Emperor's costume.

But one little boy had not heard about the new clothes. In a loud, clear voice, he shouted, "Why hasn't the Emperor got any clothes on?"

There was an awful silence. Then everyone began to laugh. "It's taken a child to show us up for the idiots we are," chuckled a man in the crowd. Soon the people were helpless with laughter and even the soldiers in the parade began to giggle behind their muskets.

Only one person was not laughing. The poor Emperor was so embarrassed, he ran straight back into the palace, with neither clothes nor dignity.

The two wicked men were never found, but the Emperor had learned his lesson. "It takes a wise man," he said, "to know when he has been really stupid."

"And you are a very, very wise man," agreed the courtiers, hiding their smiles.

# The Fisherman and His Wife

There was once a poor fisherman who lived with his wife in a hut near the shore. Neither the fisherman nor his wife cared much for housework and really the place was a disgrace. You could not go into the hut without falling over a pot or a bit of fishing line.

"What's the point of trying to keep this place clean?" grumbled the fisherman's wife. "It's not as though it would look special, whatever we do to it."

One day the fisherman went down to the sea and cast his line. Before long he felt a big tug on it and pulled, and pulled, until he had landed a huge carp. To his astonishment, the fish began to speak.

"Please, throw me back into the sea," it said. "I am no use to you, for I am not a fish at all but an enchanted Prince."

The fisherman was so amazed that he did not know what to say, but threw the fish back as it had asked.

When he got home that night, the fisherman told his wife what had happened.

"You idiot!" she cried. "You should have asked it to grant a wish, not just let it go like that. Go back and ask for a pretty little cottage instead of this miserable hut that we live in."

So the fisherman did as she said and went back to the seashore. He called out to the enchanted fish and sure enough it came swimming to the surface.

"Oh, noble fish," began the fisherman. "My wife has asked me to beg you to grant us a wish."

The fish thrashed its tail and the waves frothed and swirled. "Very well," it said. "Go home and you will find that your wish has been granted."

The fisherman hurried home and found his wife sitting happily in the neatest little cottage he had seen in his life.

"Now we want for nothing," said the fisherman happily.

"Mmmm, maybe," replied his wife.

A few weeks later, the fisherman's wife began to complain. "You know this cottage is really too small," she said. "I would much rather live in a castle. Go back and ask that fish. After all, you did save its life."

Reluctantly, the fisherman went back to the shore and called to the fish. "What do you want now?" it asked, its scales glittering in the sunshine.

The fisherman explained his wife's wish. The carp splashed angrily in the water. The sky grew dark and the waves crashed on to the beach. "Very well," said the fish. "Go home and you will find that your wish has been granted."

When the fisherman arrived home, he found his wife in gorgeous clothes ordering a whole army of servants around in a huge castle.

"Now our happiness is complete," said the fisherman.

"We'll see," replied his wife.

Only a few days later, she was complaining again. "I really think," she said, "as you saved the life of a Prince, that the least he can give us is a royal palace. He probably has dozens. It won't be a problem. I really think that you and I should have a kingdom to rule."

The fisherman argued but in the end he gave in. Against his better judgement, he made his way down to the shore and called the fish.

This time, when the fish heard what the fisherman had to say, a great storm blew up. The fisherman could hardly stay on his feet in the gusts of wind and spray. But when he went home, he found his wife in a royal palace, with a crown on her head and subjects waiting to see her. "Now, at least," he said to himself, "she cannot want for anything more."

All was well for a week or two, until the morning when the fisherman's wife woke up with a new idea in her head. "Ruling a few thousand people like this is nothing," she declared. "I want to be ruler of the world!"

The fisherman groaned and hid under the sheets. But his wife was not to be moved. With a heavy heart, he set off for the seashore.

When the fisherman told the fish what his wife wanted this time, thunder rumbled overhead. Above the crashing of the waves, the fisherman heard the fish reply:

"Go home. Your wife has what she deserves."

When the man arrived home, he found his wife back in the hut where they had started. And they are still living there to this day.

# The Frog Prince

In a land far away, there lived a King who had seven beautiful daughters. But the youngest Princess was the most beautiful, and the King loved her best of all. Unfortunately, she was also very spoiled and used to having her own way. Nothing unpleasant was allowed near her, and she did as she liked from dawn to dusk.

One day, the youngest Princess went into the woods near the royal palace and sat beneath the trees by an old well, where it was cool. As she sat, she gently threw a golden ball into the air and caught it again. But she was thinking of other things, and before she knew what was happening, the ball had fallen down the deep well.

The youngest Princess stamped her foot angrily. She was very fond of the golden ball and she hated it when things didn't go her way. She threw herself on to the ground in a tantrum and wept bitterly.

Just then, a little voice close to her ear croaked, "Princess, I can help you if you will let me."

The Princess stopped crying and looked up, only to give a little scream of horror. Sitting only two inches away from her face was a big green frog.

"Go away, you ugly, slimy creature!" cried the Princess. "How could you help *me*?"

"I could hop into the well and bring back your golden ball," explained the frog.

"What would you want in return?" asked the Princess suspiciously.

"Only to be your friend," replied the frog. "If you would sometimes play with me, and let me eat from your plate and sleep on your pillow, I will always do my best to help you."

The Princess thought for a minute. She had no intention of being friends with a *frog,* but she badly wanted to have her golden ball back. So she agreed to do what the frog had asked.

In less than a minute, the frog had jumped into the well and brought out the golden ball. He held it out to the Princess.

Carefully, so as not to touch the frog, the Princess took back the ball. Then she ran as fast as she could toward the palace. Behind her she could hear a tiny voice calling, but she paid no attention at all.

The Princess believed that she had seen the last of the frog, but that night, as she sat at supper with her father and sisters, there came a knock at the door.

"Your Highness," said a servant to the youngest Princess. "It's... er... a frog, asking for you."

"Tell him I'm busy," said the Princess quickly. "I really can't see him now."

But the King had heard the commotion and asked who was at the door. Reluctantly, the Princess told him the whole story.

"But I really cannot have a slimy green frog on the *table,*" she said, almost in tears.

The King looked sternly at her. "A promise is a promise, my dear," he said. "Go and fetch the frog at once. I should be sorry to think that any daughter of mine would go back on her word."

The Princess went slowly to the door. She took out her handkerchief and used it to pick up the frog.

"Offer our guest some food, my dear," said the King. Slowly, the Princess did as she was told.

Later that evening, when it was time to go to bed, the Princess tried to leave the frog behind in the dining room. "Aren't you forgetting something, my dear?" asked the King. She had to pick up the frog and take him to her bedroom, just as she had promised.

"Now lift me on to the pillow," begged the frog. The Princess could hardly bear it, but she did as she was told. As she placed the frog on her silken pillow, an astonishing thing happened. Before her eyes the frog turned into a handsome Prince, who sat smiling at her.

"I was bewitched by an evil enchantress," he explained. "Only the kindness of a Princess could release me from her spell."

Then the Princess was glad that she had kept her promise, for the Prince was very handsome indeed. Before many months had passed, the Prince and the Princess were married. I hear that they are always especially kind to all the green, hopping creatures in their kingdom....

# The Princess and the Pea

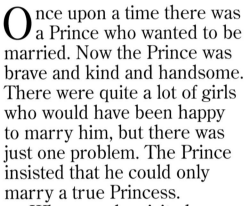

Once upon a time there was a Prince who wanted to be married. Now the Prince was brave and kind and handsome. There were quite a lot of girls who would have been happy to marry him, but there was just one problem. The Prince insisted that he could only marry a true Princess.

Whenever he visited another country, the Prince made a point of visiting all the Princesses who lived there, but he always came home without a bride.

One stormy night, the Prince was at home in the royal palace with the King and Queen. The rain poured down and the wind howled around the turrets.

Suddenly, above the rumbling of the thunder, a knock was heard at the palace door. It was so odd that someone should be out on such a night that the King himself went to see who it was.

There on the doorstep stood a lovely girl, dripping wet and shivering with cold.

"I am a Princess," said the stranger. "Please may I come in until the storm has passed?"

As soon as the Prince set his eyes on the girl, he fell head over heels in love and was determined to marry her. "After all, she *is* a Princess," he said to his mother.

"We'll see about that," said the Queen, and she hurried off to arrange for a bed to be made up for their visitor.

When the girl was shown to her room, she was surprised to see that the bed was piled high with twenty feather mattresses. But she said nothing and climbed between the sheets.

"What do you think of our young visitor?" the King asked the Queen when she returned. "Is she really a Princess?"

"We'll soon find out," smiled the Queen. "For, under the twentieth mattress of her bed, I have put a dried pea."

The next morning the royal family was having breakfast when their guest appeared.

"Did you sleep well, my dear?" asked the King, winking at the Queen.

"I'm afraid not," replied the girl. "I don't know what it was, but something lumpy in my mattress kept me awake all night."

"Then you *are* a true Princess," said the Queen. "Only a true Princess has such delicate skin."

Luckily the Princess loved the Prince as much as he loved her. They were soon married and lived happily ever after.

# The Enormous Turnip

There was once a man who had a vegetable garden that was his pride and joy. Every day he was out in his garden, digging and hoeing, weeding and watering. One day he planted two rows of turnip seeds. In no time at all, the first little leaves poked through the soil, and soon the plants were growing strongly.

But one plant was growing more strongly than all the rest! It grew and it grew and it grew, until it was the biggest turnip that anyone had ever seen.

At last the day came when the man decided to go out into his garden to pull up his turnip. He grasped hold of the leaves, counted to three and HEAVED... but he could not pull up the enormous turnip.

So the man called to his wife. "Please come and help me pull up this turnip!" he cried. His wife put her arms around his waist, and the man counted to three and... HEAVED! But they could not pull up the enormous turnip.

A little boy was passing by. "Please come and help us pull up this turnip!" cried the man and his wife. The little boy put his arms around the woman's waist. The man counted to three and... HEAVED! But they could not pull up the enormous turnip.

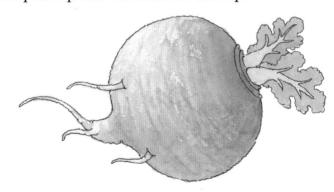

The little boy saw his sister walking by. "Come and help us pull up this turnip!" he cried. The little girl put her arms around her brother's waist. The man counted to three and... HEAVED! But they could not pull up the enormous turnip.

The little girl saw her dog by the fence. "Come and help us pull up this turnip!" she cried. The dog took hold of the little girl's skirt in his mouth. The man counted to three and... HEAVED! But they could not pull up the enormous turnip.

The dog saw a cat in a tree. "Come and help us pull up this turnip!" he barked. The cat took hold of the dog's tail. The man counted to three and... HEAVED! But they could not pull up the enormous turnip.

The cat spied a little mouse under a cabbage. "Come and help us pull up this turnip!" she meowed. The mouse took hold of the cat's tail in her mouth. The man counted to three and... HEAVED! The turnip flew out of the ground so fast that the man and the woman and the little boy and the little girl and the dog and the cat and the mouse all fell on top of each other!

The man looked at the enormous turnip and scratched his head. He still had a problem.

"Please help me to eat this enormous turnip!" he cried. So the man and the woman and the little boy and the little girl and the dog and the cat and the mouse all sat down to supper together. I wonder if they have finished eating yet?

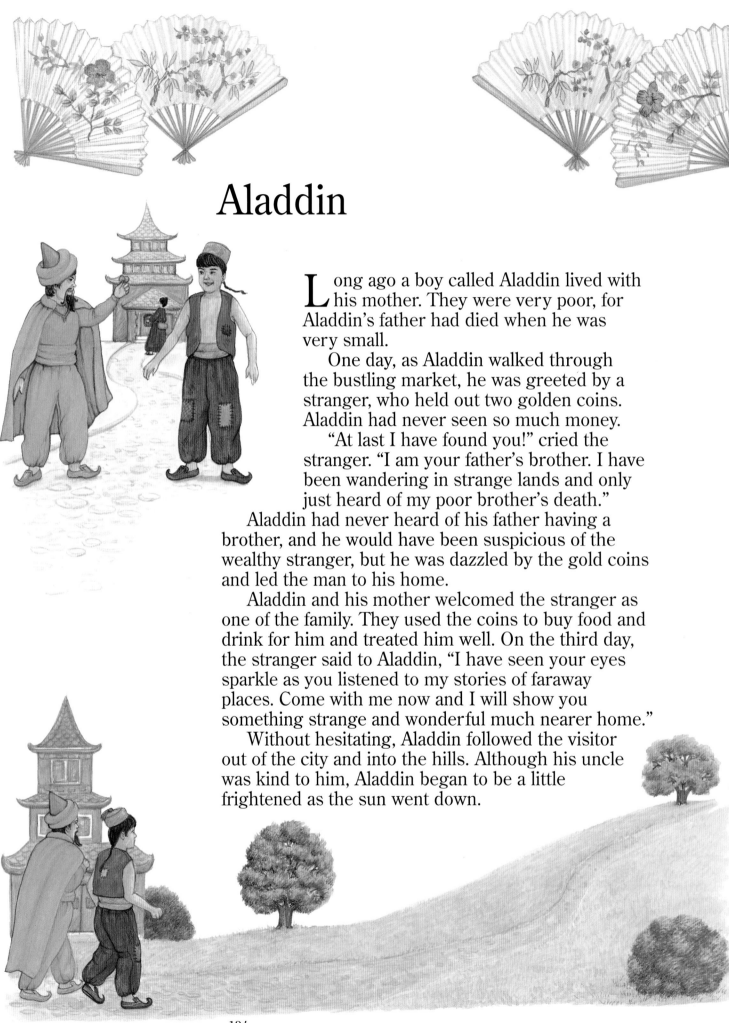

# Aladdin

Long ago a boy called Aladdin lived with his mother. They were very poor, for Aladdin's father had died when he was very small.

One day, as Aladdin walked through the bustling market, he was greeted by a stranger, who held out two golden coins. Aladdin had never seen so much money.

"At last I have found you!" cried the stranger. "I am your father's brother. I have been wandering in strange lands and only just heard of my poor brother's death."

Aladdin had never heard of his father having a brother, and he would have been suspicious of the wealthy stranger, but he was dazzled by the gold coins and led the man to his home.

Aladdin and his mother welcomed the stranger as one of the family. They used the coins to buy food and drink for him and treated him well. On the third day, the stranger said to Aladdin, "I have seen your eyes sparkle as you listened to my stories of faraway places. Come with me now and I will show you something strange and wonderful much nearer home."

Without hesitating, Aladdin followed the visitor out of the city and into the hills. Although his uncle was kind to him, Aladdin began to be a little frightened as the sun went down.

In a wooded valley, the visitor lit a fire and threw some magic powder into it. By the eerie light of the flames, Aladdin felt he was seeing the man for the first time. Far from being a kindly uncle, he was actually a wicked wizard, who needed Aladdin for a special task.

The wizard showed the terrified boy a passageway leading into the hillside. "Go down the steps," he said, "but do not touch the gold and jewels that you see. In the furthest room, you will find an old lamp. Bring that lamp to me. But first, take this ring. It will protect you."

Trembling, Aladdin did as he was told. But as he was nearing the entrance, holding the lamp he had found, Aladdin heard the wizard muttering to himself. "Ha, ha," he gloated. "Soon I will have the lamp and I can kill that stupid boy."

Aladdin wrung his hands in despair. In doing so, he rubbed the ring that the wizard had given him. All at once, there was a flash of light and an enormous genie appeared before him. "I am the genie of the ring. What is your command, O master?" he said.

"I'd like to go home," stammered Aladdin. At once it was done.

The next morning, as Aladdin slept, his mother found the old lamp. It looked in need of a good polish, so she took a rag and gave it a rub. At once, a genie towered above her. "I am the genie of the lamp," he said. "What is your command?" Aladdin was awakened by the noise. "Our troubles are over, mother," he said.

Aladdin and his mother lived very comfortably after that, but one day Aladdin chanced to catch sight of the Emperor's daughter, the Princess, and he fell deeply in love with her. Once again, he called upon the genie of the lamp to help. The genie gave him gold, jewels and a magnificent palace which so dazzled the Emperor that he agreed to his daughter's marriage to Aladdin.

Aladdin and his bride were blissfully happy, but the wicked wizard had not forgotten the lamp. He disguised himself as a lamp seller and walked through the streets, calling, "New lamps for old. New lamps for old." The Princess, anxious to please her husband, took out the old lamp and exchanged it for a new one. Immediately, the wicked wizard rubbed the lamp. With the help of the genie, he flew away to Africa, taking Aladdin's palace and the lovely Princess with him.

When Aladdin discovered what had happened, he was beside himself with grief. Then he thought to rub the wizard's ring. "What is your command, O Master?" asked the genie of the ring.

"Take me to my wife," begged Aladdin. In an instant he was by her side. The Princess was overjoyed to see her husband again and she was as clever as she was beautiful. That night she drugged the wizard's wine so that he fell into a deep sleep. Aladdin made sure that the wizard would never trouble him again. Then, with his Princess by his side, he rubbed the lamp and wished for all his former happiness to be restored to him. And so it was.

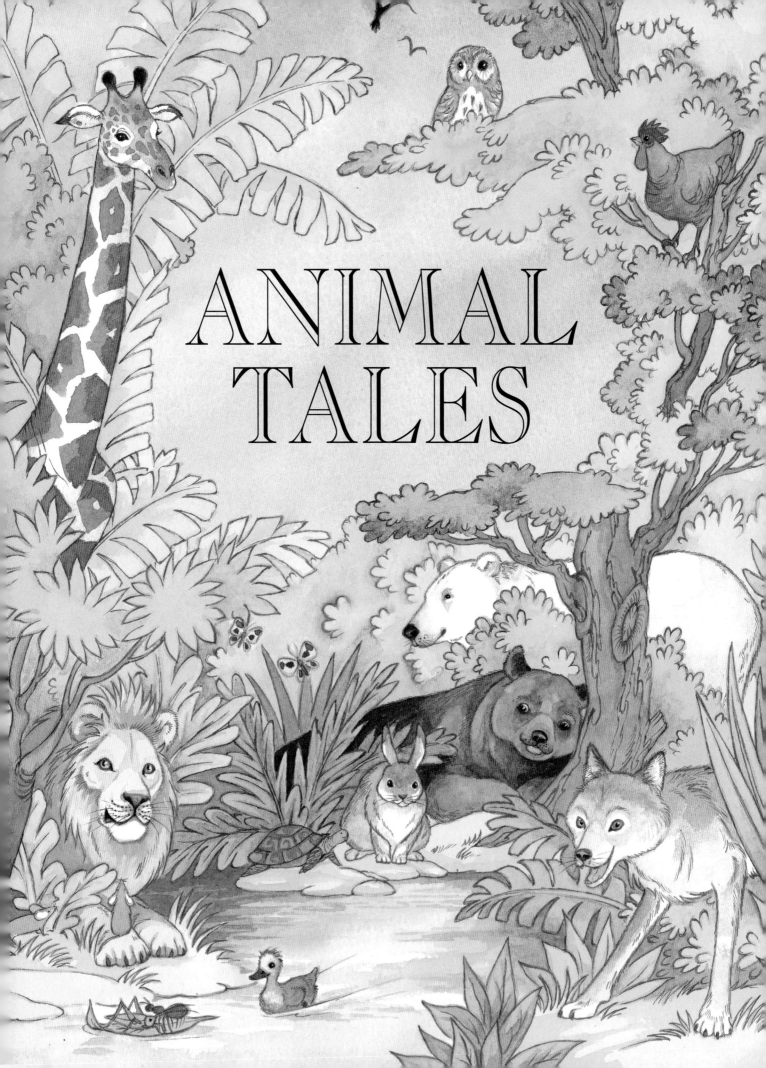

# ANIMAL TALES

# The Three Little Pigs

Once there were three little pigs, who decided that the time had come for them to set off into the wide world and find homes of their own.

"Perhaps you are right, boys," said their mother. "But remember, watch out for the big, bad wolf!"

The little pigs kissed their mother and set off. Before long they became tired and sat down to rest. Just then a farmer went past, carrying a load of straw.

"With that straw I could build a strong, safe house," said the first little pig. "You two go on without me. I will stop right here."

So the first little pig said goodbye to his brothers and bought the load of straw from the farmer. He worked very hard and soon he had built the sweetest little house you ever saw.

Meanwhile, the other two little pigs had walked a good deal farther, when they met a woodcutter carrying a load of sticks.

"With those sticks I could build a strong, safe house," said the second little pig. "You go on without me, brother. I will stop right here."

So the second little pig said goodbye to his brother and bought the load of sticks from the woodcutter. He worked even harder than the first little pig. By suppertime, he was standing outside the cutest little house you ever saw.

Meanwhile, the third little pig had walked even farther. Late that afternoon, he met a workman with a cart piled high with fine building bricks.

"With those bricks I could build a strong, safe house," said the third little pig. "I will stop right here."

So the third little pig bought the cartload of bricks from the workman and he built the nicest little brick house you ever saw.

That night the first little pig slept soundly in his straw house. But, at midnight, there came a soft tapping at the door.

"Little pig, little pig, let me come in!" called a gruff voice.

It was the big, bad wolf! The first little pig shook with fright under the sheets, but he answered the wolf bravely.

"No, no, not by the hair of my chinny chin chin, I will not let you in!"

"Then I'll huff, and I'll puff, and I'll blow your house down!" shouted the wolf. And he huffed, and he puffed, and he blew with all his might. The house of straw blew down in a moment, but the first little pig ran as fast as he could to his brother's house made of sticks.

The very next night the two little pigs were fast asleep in the house made of sticks, when there came a soft tapping on the door.

"Little pigs, little pigs, let me come in!" called a gruff voice.

You can guess who that was! The two little pigs trembled but they answered bravely.

"No, no, not by the hair of our chinny chin chins, we will not let you in!"

"Then I'll huff, and I'll puff, and I'll blow your house down!" shouted the wolf. And he huffed, and he puffed, and he blew with all his might. The house made of sticks blew down in a moment, but the two little pigs ran as fast as they could to their brother's house of bricks.

Another day passed, and the three little pigs went to sleep in the house made of bricks. In the middle of the night there came a soft tapping on the door.

"Little pigs, little pigs, let me come in!" called a gruff voice.

The three little pigs knew at once who it was but they hugged each other and answered bravely.

"No, no, not by the hair of our chinny chin chins, we will not let you in!"

"Then I'll huff, and I'll puff, and I'll blow your house down!" shouted the wolf. And he huffed, and he puffed, and he blew with all his might. But the house remained standing.

The wolf was *furious.* "If they won't let me in the door," he said to himself, "I'll climb down the chimney!"

But the third little pig heard the wolf creeping across the roof, and he quickly put a huge pot of water on the fire. When the wolf jumped down the chimney, he landed with a splash in the pot. And that was the end of the big, bad wolf!

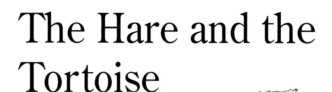

# The Hare and the Tortoise

There was once a hare who was very proud of his running. "No one is as speedy as me!" he cried. "Would anyone like to race?"

"No thanks!" laughed the other animals. "We know you can run faster than any of us. We'd be silly to try to race you."

It was the same every day. The hare would boast about his running to everyone he met and no one dared to race him.

But one fine day, a little voice piped up politely behind him. "I'll give you a race if you like, Mr. Hare," it said.

The hare turned around in surprise. Standing before him was a wrinkly old tortoise, blinking in the sunshine. "Oh, my!" replied the hare sarcastically. "You make me quake and tremble, *Mr.* Tortoise."

But the old tortoise was serious and the animals who had gathered around said, "You're always wanting to race, Mr. Hare. Let's see you do it!" So it was agreed that the hare and the tortoise would race to the old oak tree and back.

"On your marks! Get set! Go!" yelled the squirrel, waving her tail, and the runners set off.

In a couple of seconds the hare was nearly out of sight. The tortoise set off in his usual slow way. There seemed no doubt that the hare would win before the tortoise even reached the oak tree.

"Come on, Mr. Tortoise." the hare yelled over his shoulder. "This isn't much of a race!" But the tortoise saved his breath and kept plodding along,

When he reached the oak tree, the hare felt a little out of breath. For the past few months he had done more boasting than running. In any case, he knew that he was going to win easily, so he sat down under the oak tree to rest. It was a very hot day. The hare's eyelids began to close and soon he was fast asleep.

Now, all the time that the hare was dozing, the tortoise was ambling purposefully along. He took things steadily and never stopped for a rest.

An hour later, the hare woke up under the tree. He could hear cheering in the distance. Leaping to his feet, he set off as fast as his legs would carry him toward the finish line. He had never run so hard in his life. Surely he could catch the tortoise! But the tortoise's old head bobbed over the line a whisker before the hare's.

"Hurray for our new champion!" yelled all the animals.

I have heard that Mr. Hare hasn't been boasting so much lately. "Being quick on your feet is a fine thing, but slow and steady wins the race," said Mr. Tortoise.

# The Fox and the Goat

One long, hot summer, a fox wandered slowly through the countryside, pleased to see how the sun made his red coat shine. He was so busy admiring himself that he didn't notice an old well in an abandoned garden. Before he knew what was happening, he had tumbled over the edge and into the well.

Now there was not very much water in the well, so the fox was quite safe at the bottom, but the well was deep and its sides were smooth and straight. The fox quickly realized that be could not climb out again.

For several long hours, the fox paddled around and around in the shallow water at the bottom of the well. He was afraid that he would never escape.

Suddenly, the fox's gloomy thoughts were interrupted by a foolish face peering over the top of the well.

"Hello, down there!" boomed a voice. It was a goat, who had heard the splashing of the water and came to see what was happening.

The cunning fox at once saw his chance. "My friend," he called, "you have come just in time to share my good fortune. On such a hot day as this, have you ever seen anything as delightful as this cool water? I can tell you, it is quite delicious."

"But how can I reach it?" bleated the goat. "It is so far down."

"Why, jump, my friend!" cried the fox. "I promise you, you'll be quite safe. That's how I came down."

The silly goat jumped into the well, and found that the water was indeed cool and delicious. But before long, even the goat began to wonder how they could get out of the well again.

"Easy, my friend," said the fox. "Put your front feet as high up the wall as you can. I'll climb on to your back, balance on your horns, and jump to the top. Then I'll help you to get out."

Without thinking, the goat did as the fox suggested. In seconds, a grinning red face was looking down at him. "My poor friend," said the fox, "I'm afraid I can't stop to help you after all. I hope someone else comes along!" And the fox skipped off through the trees.

Like the well, the moral of this story is deep: Remember to look before you leap.

# Puss in Boots

Once upon a time there was a miller who had three sons. The miller loved his sons very much, but he was not a rich man. When he died he left his mill to the eldest son and his donkey to the middle son. All he could leave the youngest son was the cat that caught mice at the mill.

"You are a fine mouser, Puss," said the youngest son sadly. "But I don't know how that is going to help me make a living."

"Don't worry, Master," said the cat. "Just give me a pair of your old boots and a bag and you'll find that we get along very well."

The miller's son was astonished but he did as Puss asked. The clever cat put some lettuce leaves in a bag and left it in a field. When a little rabbit came out and nibbled at the leaves, Puss jumped out from his hiding place and caught the rabbit in the bag. Then he set off for the King's palace.

The servants were amazed to see a cat wearing boots, so they led him to the King.

"Your Majesty," said Puss, bowing low, "I am your loyal servant and hope that you will accept this present of a fine, plump rabbit."

The King was very amused by the cat's fine ways. "Who is your master, Puss?" he asked.

"My master is the Marquis of Carabas," said the cat grandly.

After that, the cat very often visited the King. One day he learned that the King was going to take a trip beside the river with his daughter, the Princess.

"Master," said Puss, "today you must go for a swim in the river and pretend that you have a new name. From now on, you are the Marquis of Carabas."

Later that day, the King and his daughter were riding along the riverbank in his carriage when they saw Puss running up and down in distress.

"Oh Your Majesty," cried Puss, "a terrible thing has happened. My master, the Marquis of Carabas, was swimming in the river and some thieves stole his clothes!" (In fact, Puss had hidden them in some bushes nearby.)

In no time at all the King had sent for a fine suit of clothes to be brought for the young man. When he was dressed, he was invited to ride in the royal carriage and be introduced to the Princess.

Meanwhile, Puss was running along the road ahead. When he saw some haymakers in a field, he said fiercely, "When the King comes by, if you don't say that this field belongs to the Marquis of Carabas, you'll be minced into little bits and eaten!"

The workmen were so frightened that they did just as Puss said. In fact, every field the King passed seemed to belong to the Marquis. "I congratulate you on your fine lands, my lord," said the King. The miller's son didn't know what to say, so he smiled at the Princess instead.

While this was happening, Puss had reached a huge castle. Bravely, he walked right up to the ogre that owned it.

"I've heard you can do magic, Your Giantness," said Puss. "I should so love to see some."

The ogre gave a great roar of laughter and turned himself into a lion! Puss was very frightened, but he pretended not to be.

"That's quite good," he said. "But I expect it would be more difficult for a great fellow like you to turn himself into something small like... er... a mouse?"

The ogre became a mouse in a second. But in less than a second Puss had pounced! The ogre made a very tasty snack indeed.

When the King arrived at the castle, everything was ready.

"Welcome to my master's home, Your Majesty," said Puss.

Of course, the King was very impressed, and the Princess was even more impressed. Before long she and the miller's son were married and lived happily ever after in the castle.

And Puss? Well, the castle's cellars turned out to be absolutely full of mice. So Puss lived happily ever after as well.

149

# Town Mouse and Country Mouse

Once upon a time, there was a busy little mouse who lived in the country. One morning, as he was sweeping empty nutshells from his doorway, he saw a familiar figure coming down the road. It was his cousin, who lived in the town nearby.

"Hello, cousin!" said Town Mouse. "I was getting tired of the hustle and bustle of town, so I thought I'd have a nice peaceful rest in the country."

"It would be my pleasure to have you visit," said Country Mouse. "Welcome to my home." With that, he led his cousin into his snug little house in the roots of an ancient oak tree.

But that night, Country Mouse was awakened by a forlorn little figure standing by his bed.

"Oh, cousin," said Town
Mouse. "I'm so frightened.
I couldn't get to sleep because
your straw mattress tickled me so.
And then I heard horrible rustling
and scurrying noises outside."
Country Mouse listened. "Those are just ordinary
country sounds," he said. "You'll soon get used to them."
The next day, Country Mouse got busy as usual,
picking berries and seeds to store for the winter.
"Come and help me!" he said to his cousin.
But Town Mouse didn't like hard work or getting his
hands dirty. "We have plenty of food in town, without
having to work for it," he said.

Country Mouse wanted to be kind. "I'll finish my work
and make us a picnic," he said. "You'll like that." But the
picnic was not a great success. Town Mouse was frightened
of the big cows and horses. On the way home, Country
Mouse pulled his cousin quickly into a hedge as an owl
flew by. Town Mouse made up his mind.

"I'm going home," he said, "and you must come too,
cousin. You'll love life in town. There is no work to
do and we sleep on real feather beds and eat
delicious food. You'll never want to come home."

So Country Mouse set off with Town Mouse.
After a long day's journey they reached the town and
came to the big house where Town Mouse lived.

"Isn't it splendid?" yelled Town Mouse. But Country
Mouse could hardly hear him because of the traffic.

Inside, the house was large and luxurious. "I'm
afraid of getting lost," said Country Mouse nervously.

The mice had all the food they could eat from the
pantry. But Country Mouse found it too rich. "I think
I'll go to bed now," he said. "I don't feel very well."

Tucked up between soft sheets on a feather bed,
Country Mouse was very comfortable – but he didn't
get a wink of sleep! The streetlights and the noise of
the traffic kept him awake all night.

The next morning, Town Mouse whisked Country Mouse out of the way just as a large cat was about to catch him for his breakfast! It was the last straw.

"Thank you so much for having me to stay," said Country Mouse, "but I'm going back home!"

It was a very tired little mouse who arrived back at the old oak tree that evening, but Country Mouse snuggled down on his old straw mattress with a big smile on his face. "Visiting is all very nice," he said, "but there's no place like home!"

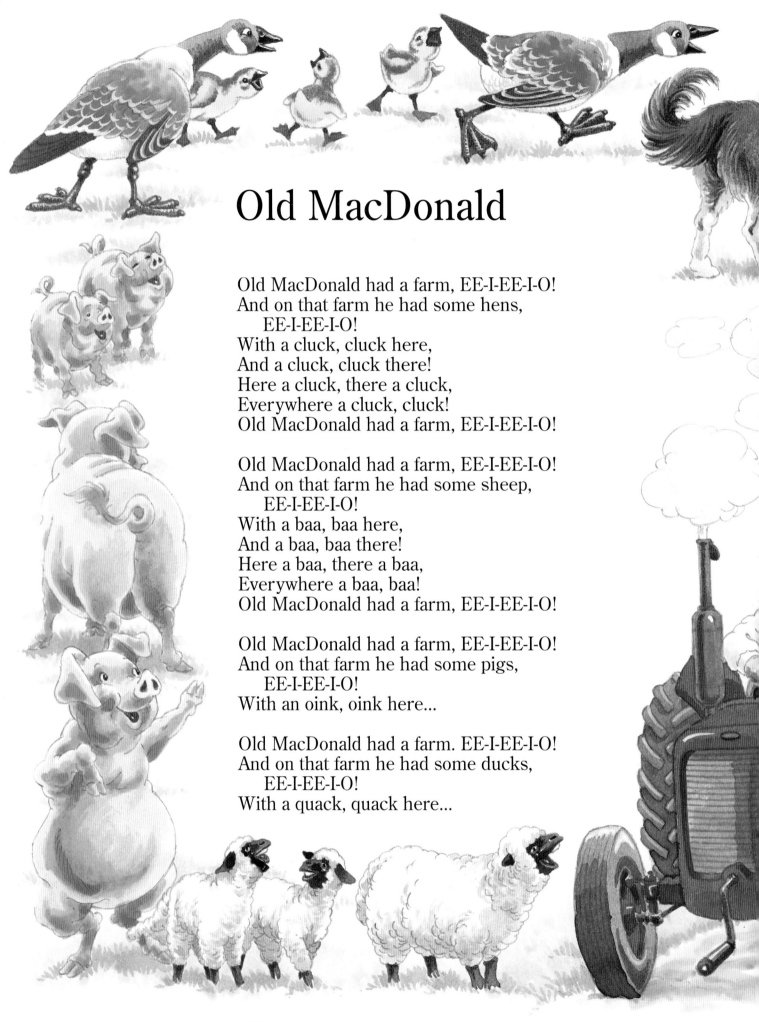

# Old MacDonald

Old MacDonald had a farm, EE-I-EE-I-O!
And on that farm he had some hens,
    EE-I-EE-I-O!
With a cluck, cluck here,
And a cluck, cluck there!
Here a cluck, there a cluck,
Everywhere a cluck, cluck!
Old MacDonald had a farm, EE-I-EE-I-O!

Old MacDonald had a farm, EE-I-EE-I-O!
And on that farm he had some sheep,
    EE-I-EE-I-O!
With a baa, baa here,
And a baa, baa there!
Here a baa, there a baa,
Everywhere a baa, baa!
Old MacDonald had a farm, EE-I-EE-I-O!

Old MacDonald had a farm, EE-I-EE-I-O!
And on that farm he had some pigs,
    EE-I-EE-I-O!
With an oink, oink here...

Old MacDonald had a farm. EE-I-EE-I-O!
And on that farm he had some ducks,
    EE-I-EE-I-O!
With a quack, quack here...

154

Old MacDonald had a farm, EE-I-EE-I-O!
And on that farm he had some cows,
    EE-I-EE-I-O!
With a moo, moo here...

Old MacDonald had a farm, EE-I-EE-I-O!
And on that farm he had some geese,
    EE-I-EE-I-O!
With a honk, honk here...

Old MacDonald had a farm, EE-I-EE-I-O!
And on that farm he had a dog,
    EE-I-EE-I-O!
With a woof, woof here...

Old MacDonald had a farm, EE-I-EE-I-O!
And on that farm he had a cat,
    EE-I-EE-I-O!
With a meow, meow here...

Old MacDonald had a farm, EE-I-EE-I-O!
And on that farm he had a tractor,
    EE-I-EE-I-O!
With a brrrm, brrrm here,
And a brrrm, brrrm there!
Here a brrrm, there a brrrm,
Everywhere a brrrm, brrrm!
Old MacDonald had a farm,
    EE-I-EE-I-O!

# The Ant and the Grasshopper

Long ago, on a sunny hillside, there lived an ant and a grasshopper. The grasshopper was a handsome insect with a glossy green coat. All day long he sat in the sun and made music, filling the hillside with his summery sounds.

The ant was a very different character. Small and dark, she bustled about every day, collecting grass seeds to store in her nest. From morning to night, she was never still.

"Why are you so silly, Ant?" asked the grasshopper lazily. "The sun is shining but you never stop to smell the flowers or look up at the sky. Life is too short to be always scurrying and hurrying."

But the ant could not be persuaded to slow down. "Summer will not last forever, Grasshopper," she said. "I must get ready for the cold winter that is coming."

"Ho ho," laughed the grasshopper. "I don't believe that winter will ever come!" and his music rang out over the hillside once more.

But soon, the leaves began to fall from the trees. The flowers died and clouds floated across the sky. It grew colder and colder. Finally, one day, feathery flakes of snow began to fall over the hillside.

The ant was snug in her nest under a stone. She had enough food for the winter. Outside, she heard a faint chirruping sound. It was the grasshopper.

"Dear Ant," he croaked. "Please give me some food. I haven't any at all stored up for myself."

But the Ant was firm. "I'm sorry, Grasshopper," she said, "but you should have thought of that before. If I give you food, I won't have enough to feed my own family."

A thick layer of snow settled over the hillside. All was still and quiet, and the music of the grasshopper was heard no more.

# The Little Red Hen

Once there was a little red hen who found some grains of wheat in a field. She carried them off to the farmyard and asked the other animals, "Who will help me to plant this wheat?"

But the cat said, "Not I!"

And the rat said, "Not I!"

And the pig said, "Not I!"

"Then I shall plant it myself," said the little red hen.

And so she did.

The days passed and the wheat began to grow. By the end of the summer it was high and golden. The little red hen went to the farmyard again and asked, "Who will help me to harvest my wheat?"

But the cat said, "Not I!"

And the rat said, "Not I!"

And the pig said, "Not I!"

"Then I shall harvest it myself," said the little red hen. And so she did.

It took the little red hen many days to cut down all the wheat and shake the grains into a big sack. When she had finished, she went back to the farmyard and asked, "Who will help me take my wheat to the miller to make it into flour?"

But the cat said, "Not I!"
And the rat said, "Not I!"
And the pig said, "Not I!"

"Then I shall take it to the mill myself," said the little red hen.

She dragged the big sack slowly to the mill and the miller ground the grain into flour.

The little red hen took her flour back to the farmyard and asked, "Who will help me take my flour to the baker to be made into bread?"

But the cat said, "Not I!"
And the rat said, "Not I!"
And the pig said, "Not I!"

"Then I shall take it to the baker myself," said the little red hen.

She went to the baker and he made four beautiful brown loaves with the flour.

The little red hen took the loaves back to the farmyard and asked, "Who would like to help me to eat my delicious bread?"

And the cat said, "I would!"
And the rat said, "I would!"
And the pig said, "I would!"

"Then I shall eat it all myself," said the little red hen. And so she did.

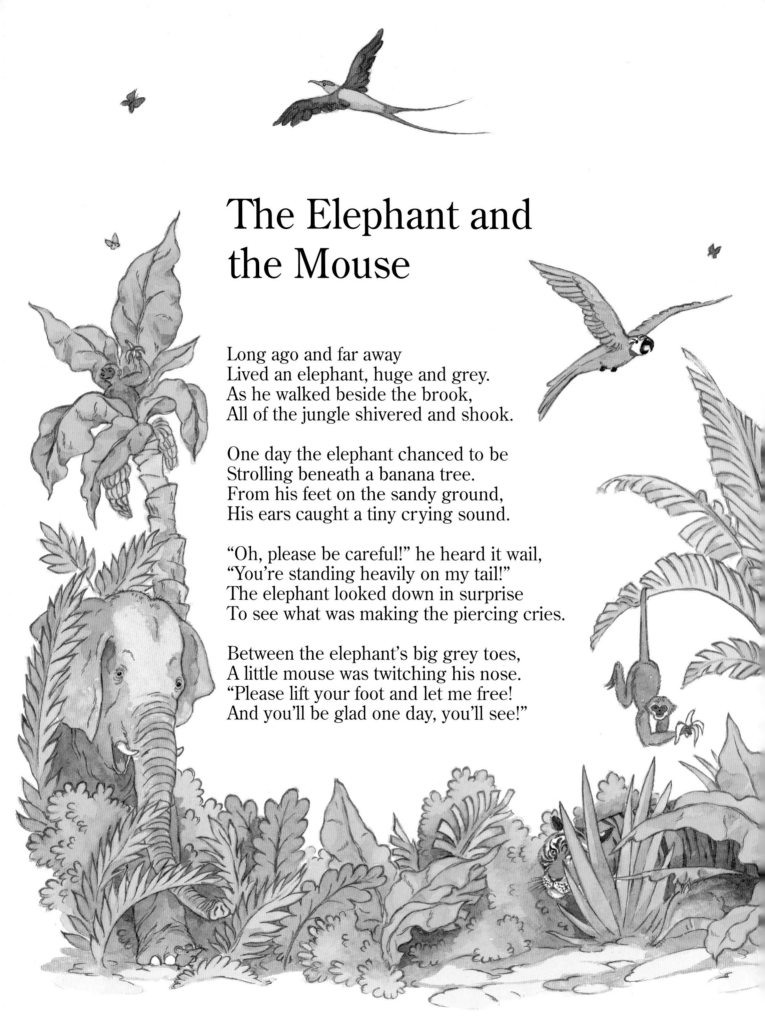

# The Elephant and
# the Mouse

Long ago and far away
Lived an elephant, huge and grey.
As he walked beside the brook,
All of the jungle shivered and shook.

One day the elephant chanced to be
Strolling beneath a banana tree.
From his feet on the sandy ground,
His ears caught a tiny crying sound.

"Oh, please be careful!" he heard it wail,
"You're standing heavily on my tail!"
The elephant looked down in surprise
To see what was making the piercing cries.

Between the elephant's big grey toes,
A little mouse was twitching his nose.
"Please lift your foot and let me free!
And you'll be glad one day, you'll see!"

Said the elephant, "Please don't be alarmed!
A fellow creature should not be harmed."
He raised his foot and the mouse ran away,
Not to be seen for many a day.

As the months passed by in the jungle heat,
The elephant gently placed his feet.
He kept his eyes upon the ground
And missed the hunters gathering round!

When he raised his head, it was far too late!
He was caught in a net, awaiting his fate.
Then a tiny voice whispered in his ear,
"Don't worry, Elephant, you've nothing to fear!"

There was the mouse from months before!
He bit into the net and began to gnaw.
In the blink of an eye, the elephant was free!
"Thank you," he said, "for rescuing me."

The moral of this story is plain to view,
If you help others, then they'll help you!

# The Wolf and the Seven Little Kids

Once upon a time, there was a mother goat who had seven little kids. One day, the mother goat had to go into the forest to find some food, but before she left, she spoke seriously to her seven little ones.

"My dears," she said. "While I am gone, you must keep the door shut and not open it to anyone. Above all, you must never open it to Mr. Wolf, because he would like to eat you for his supper. You can always tell when Mr. Wolf comes calling, no matter how he disguises himself, because he has a gruff voice and rough, hairy paws."

The little kids promised that they would be very careful, and their mother set off for the forest. But before very long, there came a knock at the door.

"My dears," said a gruff voice, "it's your mother home from the forest. Let me in!"

"You are not our mother," said the kids. "She doesn't have a gruff voice like you. Go away!"

162

At this, Mr. Wolf, for of course it was he, went to fetch a special honey drink that his granny used to make. His voice became soft and sweet. Then he hurried back to the little cottage.

"My dears," he said, in the soft voice, "it's your mother home from the forest. Let me in!" But as he spoke, he laid a paw on the window sill. "You are not our mother," cried the kids. "She doesn't have rough, hairy paws. Go away!"

At this, Mr. Wolf was very angry. He ran to the baker's shop and dipped his paws into the dough. Now he had smooth, white paws, not rough, hairy ones. Then he hurried back to the cottage and knocked on the door.

"My dears," he called. "it's your mother home from the forest. Let me in!" The little kids heard his soft voice and saw his smooth white feet on the window sill. "It *is* mother!" they cried, and they opened the door.

Immediately, Mr. Wolf came bounding in. In the blink of an eye he had gobbled up all the little kids except the smallest one of all, who hid inside the clock. After his meal, Mr. Wolf was very sleepy. He lay down under a tree and was soon snoring.

Meanwhile, the mother goat had come home. "Where are my babies?" she cried, as she saw the open front door. At last, the very smallest kid crept out of the clock and told her what had happened.

"Just wait until I find that wolf!" said the mother goat. Mr. Wolf was not hard to find because he was snoring so loudly. The mother goat looked closely at his fat tummy. She could see something moving inside! Snip! Snip! With her sewing scissors she made a little hole and out jumped the six little kids. The wolf had been so greedy that he swallowed them whole.

As Mr. Wolf slept on, the seven little kids each brought a big stone and popped it into the hole that their mother had made. Then she sewed up Mr. Wolf's tummy, and they all tiptoed away.

When Mr. Wolf woke up, he felt quite odd and very thirsty. He staggered off to drink at the well nearby.

"I thought I had swallowed six little kids," he said. "But they feel more like six big rocks in my tummy!" When Mr. Wolf got to the well, the stones in his tummy were so heavy that he toppled over and fell down into the water!

Mr. Wolf was never seen again, and the mother goat and her seven little kids lived happily ever after.

# The Ugly Duckling

There was once a mother duck who lived on a pond near a farm. All spring she sat on her nest by the bank, keeping her five big eggs warm under her feathers.

"Haven't those eggs hatched yet?" clucked a hen, as she led her fluffy chickens past the pond.

"It won't be long now," replied the mother duck sharply. "And they will be very beautiful, swimming birds when they do hatch."

Sure enough, a few days later, a faint tapping sound could be heard. One, two, three, four little fluffy ducklings hatched from the eggs. Last of all, with a squawk and a wriggle, the largest egg hatched.

The mother duck looked carefully at her fifth little duckling. He was a fine strong bird, much bigger than all the other ducklings, but there was no doubt about it: he was an ugly duckling.

"Very pretty, my dear," said the other ducks, when the mother duck took her new ducklings for their first swim. "Except for that one. *What* an ugly duckling!"

"He's just big for his age," said the mother duck. "He'll grow into his looks, you'll see."

But every day that went by, the strange duckling looked less and less like a little farm duck. The other ducks jeered at him and pecked him when his mother wasn't looking. The duckling was so unhappy that one day he ran away.

"I shall go and live with the wild ducks," he said to himself. "They won't be unkind to me."

The ugly duckling wandered until he came to the great marsh where the wild ducks lived. He saw them flying overhead and began to feel better. But the wild ducks took one look at him and began to laugh. "Go away!" they quacked. "You'll frighten our ducklings!"

So the ugly duckling ran away again. He walked wearily over fields and through woods. At last, as night was falling, he came to a cottage. He settled down on the doorstep out of the cold wind and went to sleep.

In the morning, the old woman who lived in the cottage found the sleeping duckling. "You can stay," she said kindly, "with my hen and my cat."

But the hen clucked disapprovingly. "Can you lay eggs?" she asked.

"No, I can't," squawked the ugly duckling.

"Can you purr?" asked the cat.

"Oh, no, I can't," squawked the ugly duckling.

"Then you are no use here at all," said the cat and the hen, and they chased the duckling away.

For many months the ugly duckling wandered the marshes and meadows. Later, the duckling saw some beautiful white birds flying overhead.

"If only I looked like that," he said.

The weather grew colder. One morning, the duckling woke to find the marsh had frozen. He was stuck in the ice.

Luckily, a kind farmer rescued him and took him home. The farmer's wife gave him food, and for a few days the duckling was happy. But the farmer's children chased him and wanted to play with him. The duckling grew frightened. One day he ran away again.

All winter long, the duckling lived among the reeds of the marsh. He could fly now on his long, strong wings. As he flew, he looked down at the water and saw three of the beautiful white birds below. They were swans.

"If only I could live near them, I would be happy," thought the duckling, so he flew down and landed on the clear water. As he did so, he caught sight of his own reflection and could hardly believe what he saw. He wasn't an ugly duckling at all! He was a beautiful swan, with an elegant long neck and pure white feathers.

As he landed, the other swans swam over and greeted him as though he were a long-lost friend. Proudly, the young swan swam among them. He fitted in at last.

# The Owl and the Pussycat

The Owl and the Pussycat went to sea
In a beautiful pea-green boat:
They took some honey, and plenty of money
Wrapped up in a five-pound note.
The Owl looked up to the stars above,
And sang to a small guitar,
"O lovely Pussy, O Pussy, my love,
What a beautiful Pussy you are,
　　You are,
　　You are!
What a beautiful Pussy you are!"

Pussy said to the Owl, "You elegant fowl!
How charmingly sweet you sing!
Oh! Let us be married! Too long we have tarried:
But what shall we do for a ring?"
They sailed away, for a year and a day,
To the land where the Bong-tree grows;
And there in a wood a Piggy-wig stood,
With a ring at the end of his nose,
　　His nose,
　　His nose,
With a ring at the end of his nose.

"Dear Pig, are you willing to sell for one shilling
Your ring?" Said the Piggy, "I will."
So they took it away, and were married next day
By the Turkey who lives on the hill.
They dined on mince, and slices of quince,
Which they ate with a runcible spoon;
And hand in hand, on the edge of the sand,
They danced by the light of the moon,
   The moon,
   The moon,
They danced by the light of the moon.

*Edward Lear*

# Androcles and the Lion

Long ago there lived a young man called Androcles. He was not a free man, for he was owned as a slave by a rich Roman merchant who lived in Africa. This man treated his slaves very badly; Androcles was forced to work from dawn until dusk. He had hardly any food and was often beaten cruelly. One morning, when he saw his master coming to beat him again, Androcles could bear it no longer. With the furious shouts of the merchant ringing in his ears, he ran from the house and out into the countryside.

By midday, Androcles was too tired to run any further. The African sun beat down without mercy. He looked desperately for somewhere shady to hide, and caught sight of the opening to a cave. Weak with hunger and exhaustion, Androcles crawled inside.

For a few minutes, the runaway slave rested against the cool rock wall. Suddenly, a fearsome roar echoed through the cave and a huge shape leaped toward him. It was a lion! Terrified, Androcles closed his eyes. But no attack came. Instead the slave heard a soft whimpering noise, like a lost kitten.

Androcles opened his eyes and looked at the lion. It was holding one paw off the ground. Androcles could see a large thorn buried deep in the paw, which looked sore and swollen. He hated to see a fellow creature in pain. Speaking soothingly to the huge animal, he gently pulled out the thorn.

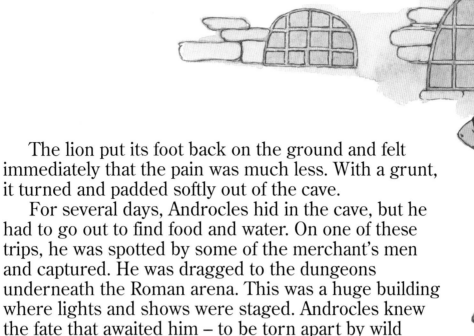

The lion put its foot back on the ground and felt immediately that the pain was much less. With a grunt, it turned and padded softly out of the cave.

For several days, Androcles hid in the cave, but he had to go out to find food and water. On one of these trips, he was spotted by some of the merchant's men and captured. He was dragged to the dungeons underneath the Roman arena. This was a huge building where lights and shows were staged. Androcles knew the fate that awaited him – to be torn apart by wild animals in front of thousands of people.

On the morning of the spectacle, two soldiers dragged Androcles from his cell and pushed him into the arena. On seats high above, Androcles could see row upon row of faces. Then the doors of the animals' cage opened and a fierce lion leaped out, roaring at the top of its voice. Androcles fell to his knees, believing that his last moments had come.

The next moment he felt a rough tongue licking his face and looked up to see the lion that he had helped standing before him. Instead of attacking him, the lion rubbed its head against him, just like a pet cat does. "So you area prisoner, too, old friend," whispered Androcles, stroking the shaggy mane.

The crowd loved this extraordinary display even more than seeing the lion tear the slave apart. They cheered and clapped, until the Roman Governor, trying to make himself more popular, announced that Androcles should be released.

Thus the slave's kindness was rewarded, and he walked away from the arena a free man at last.

# The Nightingale

Long ago, in China, there lived a great Emperor. He was richer and more powerful than any Emperor who had ever lived. His palace was as big as a city, and was beautifully decorated with silver and gold, with porcelain ornaments. Around the palace there was a garden that stretched further than the eye could see. It was full of the loveliest plants and trees. Little streams sparkled in the sun, and deep pools reflected the delicate flowers that grew along their banks. Everyone agreed that it was the most beautiful garden in the world.

Among the trees of the Emperor's garden, there lived a little brown bird who was not very beautiful at all. It was a nightingale. When the nightingale opened her mouth and sang, the notes came trickling out like pearls from a silken purse. Everyone who heard it forgot their troubles. They even forgot the beautiful garden and the powerful Emperor. They all said that the nightingale's song was the loveliest thing they had ever heard.

One day the Emperor himself was told of the nightingale's song.

"Why have I never heard this remarkable bird?" he asked. "Bring her to me at once!"

The Emperor's Chief Minister ran to the garden and explained to the nightingale that the rich and powerful Emperor wished to hear her sing.

"Gladly," said the nightingale. "Take me to the palace."

That evening, when the whole court was assembled in the throne room, the nightingale sang for the Emperor. Everyone who heard her wept at the lovely sound. As for the Emperor, he listened and the tears flowed from his eyes like diamonds.

"Put the bird in a golden cage," he cried. "I must hear this heavenly music every day."

The poor nightingale hated to be imprisoned in a cage. She grew more and more unhappy. At last she was so sad that she could not sing at all. The Emperor was furious. He ordered his wisest men to make a mechanical nightingale that would sing whenever a key was wound.

The wisest men in the kingdom worked for a year on the mechanical bird. When they had finished, they brought it before the Emperor. "This bird is even better than the real nightingale, Great Emperor," they said.

The mechanical bird was covered with gold. Precious jewels sparkled on its back and wings. When its golden key was turned, a beautiful song came from its beak. Everyone agreed that it was even better than the real nightingale. It was much more beautiful to look at and its song never changed. The real nightingale was allowed to fly back into the garden. For five years, the mechanical bird sang to the Emperor every day. But its mechanism became worn with use, and perhaps its song was not quite so beautiful as it had once been.

Then one day, the Emperor fell ill. For weeks he lay in his state chambers, growing weaker and weaker. Everyone believed that the Emperor was going to die. More and more, they left the sick man alone, while they went to pay court to the Prince who would become the new Emperor. One evening, the Emperor felt that death was very near.

Alone in his room, he longed to hear the notes of the nightingale one last time. But he was too weak to turn the golden key.

Then, from the open window, the lovely song floated into the room. The real nightingale sat on a branch outside, singing as though her heart would break.

"Sleep, my Emperor, and become strong again," she sang. "You know now that beauty cannot be caged, and gifts must be freely given."

So the Emperor slept. In the morning, when the courtiers came, expecting to find that he had died during the night, the Emperor felt better than he had done for months. Every night, the nightingale sang soothingly to him, telling him things that were valuable and true. Soon the Emperor was completely well, but he was a changed man. He ruled for many more years, and the people, who once feared him, now loved him for his kindness and wisdom.

# Peter and the Wolf

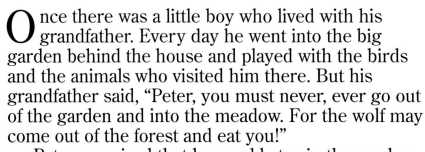

Once there was a little boy who lived with his grandfather. Every day he went into the big garden behind the house and played with the birds and the animals who visited him there. But his grandfather said, "Peter, you must never, ever go out of the garden and into the meadow. For the wolf may come out of the forest and eat you!"

Peter promised that he would stay in the garden, but secretly he thought that his grandfather was worrying about nothing. One sunny morning, he opened the garden gate and walked out into the big green meadow.

High in a tree, a little bird was singing. "Hello, Peter," she sang. "What are doing all alone in the meadow?"

"Just walking," said Peter. "You haven't seen the wolf today, have you?"

"Oh no, not today," said the bird. "When the wolf is hungry, no one is safe. Look at that duck. She has followed you from the garden. You must warn her about the wolf."

But the duck wanted to swim in the pond in the meadow. "Come and join me," she shouted to the bird. "It's lovely in here!"

"No, no, no!" chirrupped the bird. "Swimming's no good. Flying is much better," and she fluttered up and down on the bank to show how well she could fly.

But the bird didn't see that a cat was creeping through the grass behind her.

"I'll have that bird for my dinner," thought the cat. "She's too busy showing off to the duck to notice me."

Luckily, Peter turned around just at that minute. "Look out!" he called to the bird. As the cat sprang, the bird flew safely up into a tree. "Thank you, Peter," she sang.

A little later, Peter's grandfather came out into the garden. He saw that the gate was open and heard the singing and quacking and laughing coming from the meadow.

"Peter!" he shouted. "Come back into the garden at once!" Again, Peter promised not to leave the garden.

Meanwhile, out in the meadow, a shadowy shape crept out of the forest. The cat leaped up into the tree. The bird flew up and landed beside the cat. But the duck was too slow as she flapped across the grass. In a flash, the wolf had swallowed her whole! Then he prowled up and down under the tree. The cat and the bird huddled together on the branch.

Peter had seen what had happened from the garden. Suddenly, he thought of a clever plan to save the cat and the bird. "I will not be afraid of that old wolf," he said to himself.

Peter fetched a piece of rope and climbed up on to the garden wall. "Fly around the wolf's head and make him dizzy," he called to the bird. Distracted by the bird, the wolf did not see Peter tie one end of the rope to the tree and make a loop in the other end.

Then he dangled the rope down and caught the wolf by the tail! The harder the wolf pulled, the tighter the rope became. Now the wolf was feeling very sick indeed. The bird had made him dizzy and he had a very strange feeling in his tummy.

Just then some hunters came out of the forest. "Over here!" cried Peter. "We have caught the wolf!" Peter's grandfather came out to see what the noise was.

"I haven't gone out of the garden, grandfather," laughed Peter, from the top of the wall.

There was a grand procession as the hunters took the wolf to the zoo. Peter led the wolf at the end of the rope. He was happy that the wolf would be looked after and not eat the other animals any more. The bird flew overhead and the cat prowled along behind. Even the wolf was happy. He hoped that the keepers at the zoo would make the strange feeling in his tummy better.

"Quack! Quack!" Inside the wolf, the duck was feeling happier too. She stamped her feet with joy to think that she would soon be rescued. No wonder the poor wolf wasn't feeling very well!

# Noah's Ark

L ong ago, there was a very good man called Noah. He always tried to do what was right, even if it meant that his friends laughed at him.

One day, God spoke to Noah. "Everywhere, wicked people are spoiling the world and not living as they should," He said. "Only you and your family are trying to follow my laws, Noah. I am going to wash away all the wickedness in the world, but you will be saved. I want you to build a huge boat, an ark, and put on it your wife and family and two of every kind of animal on Earth."

Noah was astonished. "We live miles from the sea," he thought. "I've never built a boat in my life."

But God gave Noah instructions explaining how to build the boat, and the good man set to work.

"Going away?" jeered the people walking past. "You won't get very far in that!"

But Noah worked steadily on.

"Oh, you're building a cabin on it now," laughed the foolish people, a few weeks later. "It's a round-the-world trip, is it?"

"Well, I think it might be," said Noah thoughtfully. "You're welcome to join me if you like." But the people roared with laughter and went home.

When the ark was finished, Noah called his sons and their wives to him and asked them to help him gather up two of every kind of animal on earth.

*"Every* kind?" asked his youngest son, who did not like spiders very much.

*"Every* kind," said Noah firmly. "And we'll need to be careful that they don't eat each other."

So two by two, the animals were led to their places in the ark. The elephants nearly broke the gangplank, and the monkeys kept escaping, but at last they were all safely on board. Then Noah and his family took their places, and God shut the great doors of the ark.

People from near and far came round to laugh and joke. "Aren't you forgetting just one thing?" they asked. "What about some water to float on?"

Almost immediately, black clouds rolled across the sky and heavy rain began to fall. Once it started, it just did not stop. Day after day it fell in a steady stream.

The ark gave a lurch and a roll. "We're floating!" cried Noah. "Batten down the hatches!"

For forty days and forty nights, the ark floated on the floods. The water covered the houses and the hills. Everywhere you looked, there was only water. Huge whales and little fish swam beside the ark.

At last the rain stopped. "Soon the floods will begin to go down," said Noah. "We must find dry land."

"The sooner, the better," said his wife, for the ark was becoming just a bit smelly.

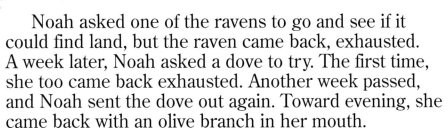

Noah asked one of the ravens to go and see if it could find land, but the raven came back, exhausted. A week later, Noah asked a dove to try. The first time, she too came back exhausted. Another week passed, and Noah sent the dove out again. Toward evening, she came back with an olive branch in her mouth.

"The water must be going down!" cried Noah. After another week, he sent the dove out for a third flight. This time she did not return. "She has found a place to build a nest," said Noah. The next day, with a bump and a jolt, the ark settled on the top of a mountain.

Joyfully, Noah and his family climbed out of the ark, and the animals followed them. There were more of them than at the beginning. Noah lifted his hands to heaven and thanked God for saving their lives.

"You have done well, Noah," said God. "I promise that I will never again send a flood to destroy the world that I have made."

And God made a rainbow that arched from the Earth to the heavens to remind us all of His promise.

# Chicken Licken

One day, as Chicken Licken was walking along, an acorn fell on his head. "Oh, my goodness," said Chicken Licken. "The sky is falling in! I must go at once and tell the King."

So Chicken Licken set off to find the King. On the way he met Henny Penny. "Where are you going, Chicken Licken?" she asked.

"The sky is falling in," said Chicken Licken, "and I am going to tell the King."

"Then I shall come too," said Henny Penny. So Chicken Licken and Henny Penny set off to find the King. On the way they met Cocky Locky.

"Where are you going to, Chicken Licken and Henny Penny?" he asked.

"The sky is falling in," cried Chicken Licken, "and we are going to tell the King."

"Then I shall come too," said Cocky Locky. So Chicken Licken and Henny Penny and Cocky Locky set off to find the King.

On the way they met Ducky Lucky. "Where are you off to, Chicken Licken, Henny Penny and Cocky Locky?" she asked.

"The sky is falling in,"cried Chicken Licken, "and we are going to tell the King."

"Then I shall come too," said Ducky Lucky.

So Chicken Licken and Henny Penny and Cocky Locky and Ducky Lucky set off to find the King.

On the way they met Drakey Lakey. "Where are you hurrying to, Chicken Licken, Henny Penny, Cocky Locky and Ducky Lucky?" he asked.

"The sky is falling in," cried Chicken Licken, "and we are going to tell the King."

"Then I shall come too," said Drakey Lakey.

So Chicken Licken, Henny Penny, Cocky Locky, Ducky Lucky and Drakey Lakey set off to find the King. On the way they met Goosey Loosey. "Where are you going so quickly, Chicken Licken, Henny Penny, Cocky Locky, Ducky Lucky and Drakey Lakey?" asked Goosey Loosey.

"The sky is falling in," cried Chicken Licken, "and we are going to tell the King."

"Then I shall come too," said Drakey Lakey.

So Chicken Licken, Henny Penny, Cocky Locky, Ducky Lucky, Drakey Lakey and Goosey Loosey set off to find the King.

On the way they met Turkey Lurkey. "Where are you going, Chicken Licken, Henny Penny, Cocky Locky, Ducky Lucky, Drakey Lakey and Goosey Loosey?" he asked.

"The sky is falling in," cried Chicken Licken, "and we are going to tell the King."

"Then I shall come too," said Turkey Lurkey.

So Chicken Licken, Henny Penny, Cocky Locky, Ducky Lucky, Drakey Lakey, Goosey Loosey and Turkey Lurkey set off to find the King. On the way they met Foxy Loxy, "Where are you off to this fine morning, my dears?" he asked.

188

"The sky is falling in," cried Chicken Licken.
"We are going to tell the King."

"Then follow me," said Foxy Loxy,
"for I know the way very well."
So Chicken Licken, Henny Penny, Cocky
Locky, Ducky Lucky, Drakey Lakey, Goosey
Loosey and Turkey Lurkey followed Foxy Loxy.
But he didn't lead them to the King. Instead he
took them to his den in the forest and there Foxy Loxy
and his wife and all his children ate Chicken Licken,
Henny Penny, Cocky Locky, Ducky Lucky, Drakey
Lakey, Goosey Loosey and Turkey Lurkey for
their breakfast!
So Chicken Licken, Henny Penny, Cocky Locky,
Ducky Lucky, Drakey Lakey, Goosey Loosey and
Turkey Lurkey never did get to see the King.
But then, the sky didn't fall in either!

# Who Killed Cock Robin?

Who killed Cock Robin?
I, said the Sparrow,
With my bow and arrow,
I killed Cock Robin.

Who saw him die?
I, said the Fly,
With my little eye,
I saw him die.

Who caught his blood?
I, said the Fish,
In my little dish,
I caught his blood.

Who'll make the shroud?
I, said the Beetle,
With my thread and needle,
I'll make the shroud.

Who'll dig his grave?
I, said the Owl,
With my pick and shovel,
I'll dig his grave.

Who'll be the parson?
I, said the Rook,
With my little book,
I'll be the parson.

Who'll be the clerk?
I, said the Lark,
If it's not in the dark,
I'll be the clerk.

All the birds of the air
Fell a-sighing and a-sobbing,
When they heard the bell toll
For poor Cock Robin.

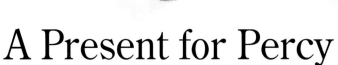

# A Present for Percy

It's easy to buy a good present
For someone who's active and fun.
You find what they need for their hobbies
And buy the most suitable one.

But what do you buy for a piglet
Who spends all the time in his chair?
He only gets up when he's hungry,
And even that's getting quite rare!

You can't buy him socks or a sweater,
It really can make you depressed,
    He just watches his big television
        And most days he doesn't get dressed!

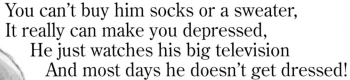

One Christmas his cousin Belinda
Gave Percy an exercise tape.
"Just ten minutes a day," she said, "Percy,
You'll soon be in wonderful shape!"

A month or two later, Belinda
Asked, "Are you using the tape as you should?"
Said Percy, "I find that I don't have to move,
Just watching it through does me good!"

So we've all given up on young Percy,
For buying him gifts is no fun.
Perhaps he'll do something dynamic
When this year he doesn't get one!

# The Three
# Billy Goats Gruff

Once there were three billy goats called Gruff. They lived in the mountains, scrambling over rocks and streams in search of the fresh, green grass they loved. One day the three billy goats Gruff stood on a hillside and looked down into the next valley.

"That is the greenest grass I have seen for many a day," said the biggest billy goat, "but how can we reach it?"

Between the billy goats and the fresh, green grass, a wide river rushed along. It was far too wide and fast-flowing for the billy goats to swim across.

"We will walk along the bank," said the middle-sized billy goat, "until we come to a place where we can cross safely."

194

So the billy goats walked
along the riverbank until they came to a
narrow wooden bridge.

"No one seems to use the bridge, perhaps it is not
very strong," said the smallest billy goat.

"I am the lightest, so I will go first to make sure."

In fact the bridge was strong and safe but a wicked old
troll lived underneath it. Whenever he heard footsteps on
the bridge, he jumped out and ate anyone who tried to cross.

The smallest billy goat Gruff did not know this. *Trip, trap,
trip, trap,* went his hooves on the wooden planks. Suddenly
the ugly old troll's face popped over the edge of the bridge.

"Who's that trip-trapping across *my* bridge?" he roared.

The little goat was almost too frightened to speak, but at
last he said, "I'm the smallest billy goat Gruff."

"Well, I'm a troll, and I'm going to eat you for my dinner!"

"Oh, don't do that," said the smallest billy goat
Gruff. "My brother is following me and he is much
fatter than I am. He will make you a much
better dinner than me."

The troll thought for a
minute. The little goat looked
very tasty, but a bigger goat would
be better still. So he let the smallest billy
goat Gruff go trip-trapping on across the bridge
and on to the fresh, green grass on the other side.

When the middle-sized goat saw his brother
jumping and running on the other side of the bridge,
he decided to cross the bridge himself. *Trip, trap, trip,
trap* went his hooves on the wooden planks. In the very
middle of the bridge, the ugly old troll popped up again.
"Who's that trip-trapping across my bridge?" he roared.

The middle-sized billy goat Gruff was also very
frightened. He knew how much trolls love to eat fat
mountain goats, but he answered bravely. "Oh, I'm
the middle-sized billy goat Gruff," he said, "but you
don't want to trouble yourself with me. My elder
brother is following me and he will make a much
better meal for a big, strong troll like you."

The greedy troll thought for a minute. Then he let the middle-sized goat go trip-trapping over the bridge, to run in the fresh, green grass on the other side.

Now the biggest billy goat Gruff had seen everything that had happened and he smiled to himself. His big hooves went *trip, trap, trip, trap,* on the wooden planks. It wasn't long before the troll jumped right out of his hiding place and stood in the middle of the bridge.

"Who's that trip-trapping across *my* bridge?" he roared, louder than ever.

"I'm the biggest billy goat Gruff," came the reply. "Move out of my way!"

"Oh no," said the troll with an ugly sneer. "I've been waiting all morning for this. I'm going to eat you for my dinner!"

But the biggest billy goat Gruff set off down the bridge at a run. *TRIP, TRAP, TRIP, TRAP* went his mighty hooves. When he reached the middle of the bridge, he lowered his horns and CHARGED!

With a great roar, the ugly old troll flew high up into the air, then he fell with a huge splash into the river below. The fast-flowing water carried him far away, never to be seen again.

And the three billy goats Gruff found all the fresh, green grass they could wish for in the valley, and lived happily ever after.

# The Sly Fox and the Little Red Hen

Once there was a little red hen who lived by herself in the woods. She had a compact little house, which she kept very clean. Her house kept her warm in the winter and safe at night from the sly fox, who lived nearby with his mother.

One morning the little red hen went into the woods to collect some sticks for her fire. She worked hard and pretty soon she had a large bundle to carry home. But she didn't know that the sly young fox had been watching her all this time. When he saw that the little red hen was ready to go home, he ran quickly ahead of her and slipped into the little house. In a flash, he had hidden himself behind the little red hen's strong front door.

The little red hen hurried up the steps to her house and carried her sticks inside. But the moment she shut the door, the sly young fox jumped out at her. Squawking with terror, the little red hen flew up to the roof and perched on one of the rafters. She thought that she would be safe there.

The sly young fox laughed to himself. "You can't escape from me so easily, Little Red Hen!" he said, and he began to behave in a very strange way.

"Whatever is he *doing*? said the little red hen to herself, as the fox chased his own tail around and around the room. She watched and watched until she became so dizzy that she dropped right off her perch.

Of course, that was just what the sly young fox had planned. He picked up the little red hen and popped her into a sack he had brought with him. "You will make a very fine dinner for my mother and me," he said, as he tied up the sack and set off back to his den in the woods.

The little red hen kept very quiet in the sack. She was thinking hard and wondering if she would soon have a chance to escape.

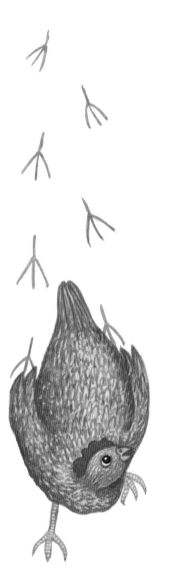

Pretty soon the fox became tired after all his watching, and waiting, and chasing.

He lay down near some rocks and went to sleep. When she heard him snoring, the little red hen pecked at the bag and made a hole near the top, one just big enough for her to escape. Then she quietly gathered some large stones and put them into the sack. At last she tiptoed away and ran all the way back to her snug little house.

When the sly young fox woke up, he set off once more. "The little red hen feels even heavier than before," he said to himself. "I hope that my mother has a big pot of water boiling on the stove to cook this tasty little bird."

When he reached his den, the fox's mother was delighted. "The water is boiling, my clever boy," she said. "Throw the hen in at once."

The fox and his mother leaned over the pot as he untied the sack and turned it upside down. With an enormous splash, the stones fell into the boiling water!

The water splashed all over the two foxes and gave them the fright of their lives. They limped away from the woods and were never seen again.

The little red hen lived happily ever after, but she was always sure to lock her door when she went out!

# NURSERY RHYMES

Old Mother Goose,
When she wanted to wander,
Would ride through the air
On a very fine gander.

Mother Goose had a house,
'Twas built in a wood,
An owl at the door
For a porter stood.

She had a son Jack,
A plain-looking lad,
He was not very good,
Nor yet very bad.

She sent him to market,
A live goose he bought:
"Here! Mother," says he,
"It will not go for naught."

Jack's goose and her gander
Grew very fond;
They'd both eat together,
Or swim in one pond.

Jack found one morning,
As I have been told,
His goose had laid him
An egg of pure gold.

Jack rode to his mother,
The news for to tell.
She called him a good boy,
And said it was well.

"Cackle, cackle, Mother Goose,
Have you any feathers loose?"
"Truly I have, my pretty fellow,
Half enough to fill a pillow.
Here are quills,
Take one or two,
And down to make
A bed for you."

Little Boy Blue,
Come blow your horn,
The sheep's in the meadow,
The cow's in the corn.

But where is the boy
Who looks after the sheep?
He's under the haystack,
Fast asleep!

Will you wake him?
No, not I!
For if I do,
He's sure to cry.

Little Bo-Peep
Has lost her sheep,
And doesn't know where to find them.
Leave them alone,
And they'll come home,
Wagging their tails behind them.

I had a little nut tree,
Nothing would it bear
But a silver nutmeg
And a golden pear.

The King of Spain's daughter
Came to visit me,
And all for the sake
Of my little nut tree.

A swarm of bees in May
Is worth a load of hay;
A swarm of bees in June
Is worth a silver spoon;
A swarm of bees in July
Is not worth a fly.

All things bright and beautiful,
All creatures great and small,
All things wise and wonderful,
The Lord God made them all.

Jack and Jill went up the hill,
To fetch a pail of water.
Jack fell down and broke his crown,
And Jill came tumbling after.

Up Jack got and home did trot,
As fast as he could caper.
He went to bed to mend his head
With vinegar and brown paper.

Mary, Mary, quite contrary,
How does your garden grow?
With silver bells,
And cockle-shells,
And pretty maids all in a row.

Curly Locks, Curly Locks,
Wilt thou be mine?
Thou shalt not wash dishes,
Nor yet feed the swine;
But sit on a cushion
And sew a fine seam,
And feed upon strawberries, sugar and cream.

Hickory, dickory, dock,
The mouse ran up the clock.
The clock struck one,
The mouse ran down,
Hickory, dickory, dock.

Six little mice sat down to spin;
Pussy passed by, and she peeped in.
"What are you doing, my little men?"
"Weaving coats for gentlemen."
"Shall I come in and cut off your threads?"
"No, no, Mistress Pussy, you'd bite off
    our heads."
"Oh no, I won't, I'll help you spin."
"That may be so, but you can't come in!"

Oh, the grand old Duke of York,
He had ten thousand men;
He marched them up to the top of the hill,
And he marched them down again.

And when they were up, they were up,
And when they were down, they were down,
And when they were only halfway up,
They were neither up nor down.

For want of a nail, the shoe was lost,
For want of a shoe, the horse was lost,
For want of a horse, the rider was lost,
For want of a rider, the battle was lost,
For want of a battle, the kingdom was lost,
And all for the want of a horseshoe nail.

The lion and the unicorn
Were fighting for the crown;
The lion beat the unicorn
All around the town.

Some gave them white bread,
And some gave them brown;
Some gave them plum-cake,
And drummed them out of town.

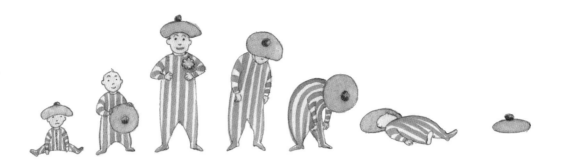

Solomon Grundy,
Born on Monday,
Christened on Tuesday,
Married on Wednesday,
Took ill on Thursday,
Worse on Friday,
Died on Saturday,
Buried on Sunday,
And that was the end
Of Solomon Grundy.

Old King Cole was a merry old soul,
And a merry old soul was he;
He called for his pipe,
And he called for his bowl,
And he called for his fiddlers three.

Every fiddler, he had a fiddle,
And a very fine fiddle had he
(Twee tweedle dee, tweedle dee, went the fiddlers.)
Oh there's none so rare
As can compare
With King Cole and his fiddlers three.

Georgie Porgie,
Pudding and pie,
Kissed the girls
And made them cry.
When the boys
Came out to play,
Georgie Porgie
Ran away.

Doctor Foster went to Gloucester
In a shower of rain;
He stepped in a puddle,
Right up to his middle,
And never went there again.

One, two, buckle my shoe;
Three, four, knock on the door;
Five, six, pick up sticks;
Seven, eight, lay them straight;
Nine, ten, my fat hen;
Eleven, twelve, dig and delve;
Thirteen, fourteen, maids a-courting;
Fifteen, sixteen, maids in the kitchen;
Seventeen, eighteen, maids in waiting;
Nineteen, twenty, my plate's empty.

Tinker, tailor, soldier, sailor,
Rich man, poor man, beggar man, thief.

Where are you going to, my pretty maid?
I'm going a-milking, sir, she said.
May I come with you, my pretty maid?
Yes, if you like, kind sir, she said.

What is your fortune, my pretty maid?
My face is my fortune, sir, she said.
Then I cannot marry you, my pretty maid.
Nobody asked you, sir, she said.

Oranges and lemons,
Say the bells of St. Clement's.

You owe me five farthings,
Say the bells of St. Martin's.

When will you pay me?
Say the bells of Old Bailey.

When I grow rich,
Say the bells of Shoreditch.

When will that be?
Say the bells of Stepney.

I'm sure I don't know,
Says the great bell of Bow.

London Bridge is falling down,
Falling down, falling down,
London Bridge is falling down,
My fair lady.

Build it up with wood and clay,
Wood and clay, wood and clay,
Build it up with wood and clay,
My fair lady.

Wood and clay will wash away,
Wash away, wash away,
Wood and clay will wash away,
My fair lady.

Build it up with strongest stone,
Strongest stone, strongest stone,
Build it up with strongest stone,
My fair lady.

Little Jack Horner
Sat in a corner,
Eating his Christmas pie.
He put in his thumb
And pulled out a plum,
And said, "What a good boy am I!"

Jack Spratt could eat no fat,
His wife could eat no lean,
And so between them both, you see,
They licked the platter clean.

Yankee Doodle came to town,
Riding on a pony;
He stuck a feather in his cap
And called it macaroni.

Little Tommy Tucker
Sings for his supper;
What shall we give him?
Brown bread and butter.
How shall he cut it
Without a knife?
How will he be married
Without a wife?

Tom, Tom, the piper's son,
He learned to play when he was young,
And all the tune that he could play
Was "Over the hills and far away"
Over the hills and a great way off,
The wind shall blow my topknot off.

Tom, Tom, the piper's son,
Stole a pig and away did run;
The pig was eat
And Tom was beat,
And Tom went howling down the street.

The man in the moon
Came down too soon
And asked the way to Norwich;
He went by the south
And burned his mouth
By eating cold plum porridge.

Hot cross buns!
Hot cross buns!
One a penny,
Two a penny,
Hot cross buns!
If you have no daughters,
Give them to your sons,
One a penny,
Two a penny,
Hot cross buns!

Pease porridge hot,
Pease porridge cold,
Pease porridge in the pot,
Nine days old.
Some like it hot,
Some like it cold,
Some like it in the pot,
Nine days old.

Little Miss Muffet
Sat on a tuffet,
Eating her curds and whey.
Along came a spider,
Who sat down beside her,
And frightened Miss Muffet away.

Incy Wincy Spider
Climbed up the water spout,
Down came the rain
And washed the spider out!

Out came the sun
That dried up all the rain,
So Incy Wincy Spider
Climbed up the spout again!

There was a crooked man,
And he walked a crooked mile,
He found a crooked sixpence
Upon a crooked stile;
He bought a crooked cat,
Which caught a crooked mouse,
And they all lived together
In a little crooked house.

It's raining, it's pouring,
The old man is snoring.
He went to bed
And bumped his head,
And couldn't get up in the morning!

Sing a song of sixpence,
A pocket full of rye;
Four and twenty blackbirds,
Baked in a pie.

When the pie was opened,
The birds began to sing;
Wasn't that a dainty dish
To set before the King?

The King was in his counting-house,
Counting out his money;
The Queen was in the parlour
Eating bread and honey.

The maid was in the garden,
Hanging out the clothes,
When down came a blackbird
And pecked off her nose!

The Queen of Hearts
She made some tarts,
All on a summer's day;
The Knave of Hearts
He stole the tarts,
And took them right away.

The King of Hearts
Called for the tarts,
And beat the Knave full sore;
The Knave of Hearts
Brought back the tarts,
And vowed he'd steal no more.

Bobby Shafto's gone to sea,
Silver buckles on his knee;
He'll come home and marry me,
Bonny Bobby Shafto!

Bobby Shafto's bright and fair,
Combing down his yellow hair,
He's my love forever more,
Bonny Bobby Shafto!

I saw a ship a-sailing,
A-sailing on the sea,
And oh, but it was laden
With pretty things for thee!

There were comfits in the cabin
And apples in the hold;
The sails were made of silk
And the masts were all of gold!

The four and twenty sailors
Who stood between the decks
Were four and twenty white mice
With chains about their necks.

The captain was a duck
With a packet on his back,
And when the ship began to move,
The captain said, "Quack! Quack!"

See-saw, Margery Daw,
Johnny shall have a new master;
He shall have but a penny a day,
Because he can't work any faster!

Humpty Dumpty sat on a wall,
Humpty Dumpty had a great fall.
All the King's horses
And all the King's men
Couldn't put Humpty together again.

Here we go 'round the mulberry bush,
The mulberry bush, the mulberry bush,
Here we go 'round the mulberry bush,
On a cold and frosty morning!

This is the way we wash our clothes,
Wash our clothes, wash our clothes,
This is the way we wash our clothes,
On a cold and frosty morning.

Ring-a-ring-a-roses,
A pocket full of posies.
A-tishoo! A-tishoo!
We all fall down!

To market, to market, to buy a fat pig,
Home again, home again, jiggety jig.
To market, to market, to buy a fat hog,
Home again, home again, jiggety jog.

This little piggy went to market,
This little piggy stayed at home,
This little piggy had roast beef,
This little piggy had none.
And this little piggy cried,
"Whee, whee, whee," all the way home!

230

There was an old woman who lived in a shoe,
She had so many children she didn't know what to do.
She gave them some broth without any bread,
And scolded them soundly and sent them to bed.

Girls and boys, come out to play,
The moon doth shine as bright as day.
Leave your supper and leave your sleep,
And come to your playfellows in the street.
Come with a whoop, and come with a call,
Come with a good will, or not at all.
Come let us dance on the open green,
And she who holds longest shall be our queen.

231

Old Mother Hubbard
Went to the cupboard
To fetch her poor dog a bone.
But when she got there,
The cupboard was bare,
And so the poor dog had none.

She sent to the baker's
To buy him some bread;
But when she came back,
The poor dog was dead.

She went to the undertaker's
To buy him a coffin;
But when she came back,
The poor dog was laughing.

She took a clean dish
To get him some tripe;
But when she came back,
He was smoking a pipe.

She went to the alehouse
To get him some beer;
But when she came back,
The dog sat in a chair.

She went to the tavern
For white wine and red;
But when she came back,
The dog stood on his head.

She went to the grocer's
To buy him some fruit,
But when she came back,
He was playing the flute.

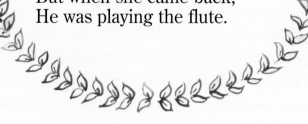

She went to the tailor's
To buy him a coat;
But when she came back,
He was riding a goat.

She went to the hatter's
To buy him a hat;
But when she came back,
He was feeding the cat.

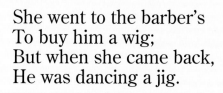

She went to the barber's
To buy him a wig;
But when she came back,
He was dancing a jig.

She went to the cobbler's
To buy him some shoes;
But when she came back,
He was reading the news.

She went to the seamstress
To buy him some linen;
But when she came back,
The dog was a-spinning.

She went to the hosier's
To buy him some hose;
But when she came back,
He was dressed in his clothes.

The dame made a curtsy,
The dog made a bow;
The dame said, "Your servant,"
The dog said, "Bow-wow!"

Mary had a little lamb,
Its fleece was white as snow;
And everywhere that Mary went,
The lamb was sure to go.

It followed her to school one day,
Which was against the rule;
It made the children laugh and play
To see a lamb at school.

And so the teacher turned it out,
But still it lingered near;
And waited patiently about,
'Til Mary did appear.

"Why does the lamb love Mary so?"
The eager children cry;
"Why, Mary loves the lamb, you know,"
The teacher did reply.

Baa, baa, black sheep,
Have you any wool?
Yes, sir, yes, sir,
Three bags full.
One for the master,
And one for the dame,
And one for the little boy
Who lives down the lane.

The north wind doth blow,
And we shall have snow,
And what will poor Robin do then,
Poor thing?

He'll sit in a barn,
And keep himself warm,
And hide his head under his wing,
Poor thing.

A wise old owl lived in an oak;
The more he saw, the less he spoke;
The less he spoke, the more he heard.
Why can't we all be like that wise old bird?

Polly, put the kettle on,
Polly, put the kettle on,
Polly, put the kettle on,
We'll all have tea.

Sukey, take it off again,
Sukey, take it off again,
Sukey, take it off again,
They've all gone away.

Blow the fire and make the toast,
Put the muffins on to roast,
Who is going to eat the most?
We'll all have tea.

Pat-a-cake, pat-a-cake, baker's man,
Bake me a cake as fast as you can;
Pat it and prick it and mark it with B,
And put it in the oven for baby and me.

Simple Simon met a pieman
Going to the fair;
Said Simple Simon to the pieman,
"Let me taste your wares."

Said the pieman to Simple Simon,
"Show me first your penny."
Said Simple Simon to the pieman,
"Indeed, I haven't any."

Simple Simon went a-fishing,
For to catch a whale;
All the water he had got
Was in his mother's pail.

Simple Simon went to look
If plums grew on a thistle;
He pricked his finger very much,
Which made poor Simon whistle.

Oh, dear, what can the matter be?
Dear, dear, what can the matter be?
Oh, dear, what can the matter be?
Johnny's so long at the fair.

He promised to buy me a bunch of blue ribbons,
He promised to buy me a bunch of blue ribbons,
He promised to buy me a bunch of blue ribbons,
To tie up my bonny brown hair.

As I was going to St. Ives,
I met a man with seven wives.
Each wife had seven sacks,
Each sack had seven cats,
Each cat had seven kits.
Kits, cats, sacks and wives,
How many were going to St. Ives?

(Only one – the man and his wives were going the other way!)

Half a pound of tuppenny rice,
Half a pound of treacle,
Mix it up and make it nice,
Pop goes the weasel!

Up and down the City Road,
In and out the Eagle,
That's the way the money goes,
Pop goes the weasel!

Ride a cock-horse to Banbury Cross
To see a fine lady upon a white horse.
With rings on her fingers and bells on her toes,
She shall have music wherever she goes!

I had a little pony,
His name was Dapple Grey;
I loaned him to a lady,
To ride a mile away.
She whipped him,
She slashed him,
She rode him through the mire;
I would not lend my pony now,
For all the lady's hire.

How many miles to Babylon?
Three score miles and ten.
Can I get there by candlelight?
Yes, and back again.
If your heels are nimble and light,
You may get there by candlelight.

Jack, be nimble,
Jack, be quick,
Jack, jump over the candlestick!

Higgledy, piggledy, my black hen,
She lays eggs for gentlemen;
Gentlemen come every day
To see what my black hen doth lay.
Sometimes nine and sometimes ten,
She lays eggs for gentlemen.

Goosey, goosey, gander,
Whither shall I wander?
Upstairs, downstairs,
And in my lady's chamber.

There I met an old man,
Who wouldn't say his prayers.
So I took him by the left leg
And threw him down the stairs.

Cock-a-doodle-doo!
My dame has lost her shoe!
My master's lost his fiddling stick
And doesn't know what to do!

Cock-a-doodle-doo!
What is my dame to do?
'Till master finds his fiddling stick,
She'll dance without her shoe!

Cock-a-doodle-doo!
My dame has found her shoe.
And master's found his fiddling stick,
Sing doodle-doodle-doo!

Cock-a-doodle-doo!
My dame will dance with you.
While master fiddles his fiddling stick
For dame and doodle-doo.

I love little pussy,
Her coat is so warm,
And if I don't hurt her
She'll do me no harm.
So I'll not pull her tail,
Nor drive her away,
But pussy and I
Very gently will play.

Hey, diddle, diddle,
The cat and the fiddle,
The cow jumped over the moon.
The little dog laughed
To see such sport,
And the dish ran away with the spoon.

Ding, dong, bell,
Pussy's in the well.
Who put her in?
Little Johnny Green.
Who pulled her out?
Little Tommy Stout.
What a naughty boy was that
To try to drown poor pussycat,
Who never did him any harm
But killed all the mice in his father's barn.

Pussycat, pussycat, where have you been?
I've been up to London to look at the Queen.
Pussycat, pussycat, what did you there?
I frightened a little mouse under her chair.

Little Tommy Tittlemouse
Lived in a little house;
He caught fishes
In other men's ditches.

Lucy Locket lost her pocket,
Kitty Fisher found it.
Not a penny was there in it
But a ribbon 'round it.

Little Polly Flinders
Sat among the cinders,
Warming her pretty little toes;
Her mother came and caught her,
And whipped her little daughter
For spoiling her nice new clothes.

Tweedledum and Tweedledee
Agreed to have a battle;
For Tweedledum said Tweedledee
Had spoiled his nice new rattle.
Just then flew down a monstrous crow,
As black as a tar-barrel,
Which frightened both the heroes so,
They quite forgot their quarrel.

*Lewis Carroll*

Peter, Peter, pumpkin eater,
Had a wife and couldn't keep her;
He put her in a pumpkin shell,
And there he kept her very well.

Peter, Peter, pumpkin eater,
Had another and didn't love her;
Peter learned to read and spell,
And then he loved her very well.

Lavender's blue, dilly, dilly,
Lavender's green;
When I am King, dilly, dilly,
You shall be Queen.

Call up your men, dilly, dilly,
Set them to work,
Some to the plough, dilly, dilly,
Some to the cart.

Some to make hay, dilly, dilly,
Some to thresh corn,
While you and I, dilly, dilly,
Keep ourselves warm.

248

Rub-a-dub-dub,
Three men in a tub,
And how do you think they got there?
The butcher, the baker,
The candlestick-maker,
They all jumped out of a rotten potato,
'Twas enough to make a man stare!

Three wise men of Gotham,
They went to sea in a bowl,
And if the bowl had been stronger,
My song had been longer.

Dance to your Daddy,
My little laddie,
Dance to your Daddy,
My little lamb!
You shall have a fishy
On a little dishy,
You shall have a fishy
When the boat comes in.

Dance to your Daddy,
My little laddie,
Dance to your Daddy,
My little lamb!
You shall have an apple,
You shall have a plum,
You shall have a rattle-basket,
When your Dad comes home.

Pretty maid, pretty maid,
Where have you been?
Gathering roses
To give to the Queen.
Pretty maid, pretty maid,
What gave she you?
She gave me a diamond
As big as my shoe.

Monday's child is fair of face,
Tuesday's child is full of grace,
Wednesday's child is full of woe,
Thursday's child has far to go,
Friday's child is loving and giving,
Saturday's child works hard for a living,
But the child that is born on the Sabbath day
Is bonny and blithe, and good, and gay.

Three blind mice,
See how they run!
They all ran after the farmer's wife,
Who cut off their tails with a carving knife,
Did ever you see such a thing in your life,
As three blind mice?

A cat came fiddling out of a barn,
With a pair of bagpipes under her arm;
She could sing nothing but "Fiddle-de-dee,
The mouse has married the bumble bee."
Pipe, cat; dance, mouse;
We'll have a wedding at our good house.

Three little kittens, they lost their mittens,
And they began to cry,
"Oh mother dear, we sadly fear
That we have lost our mittens."
"What! Lost your mittens, you naughty kittens?
Then you shall have no pie.
Mee-ow, mee-ow, mee-ow,
No, you shall have no pie."

The three little kittens they found their mittens
And they began to cry,
"Oh mother dear, see here, see here,
For we have found our mittens."
"Put on your mittens, you silly kittens,
And you shall have some pie."
Purr-r, purr-r, purr-r,
Oh, let us have some pie.

The three little kittens put on their mittens
And soon ate up the pie.
"Oh mother dear, we greatly fear
That we have soiled our mittens."
"What! Soiled your mittens, you naughty kittens?"
Then they began to sigh,
Mee-ow, mee-ow, mee-ow,
Then they began to sigh.

The three little kittens they washed their mittens
And hung them out to dry.
"Oh! Mother dear, do you not hear
That we have washed our mittens?"
"What! washed your mittens,
    you good little kittens?
But I smell a rat close by."
  Mee-ow, mee-ow, mee-ow,
    We smell a rat close by.

I see the moon,
And the moon sees me.
God bless the moon,
And God bless me.

Star light, star bright,
First star I see tonight,
I wish I may, I wish I might,
Have the wish I wish tonight.

Wee Willie Winkie runs through the town,
Upstairs and downstairs, in his nightgown.
Rapping at the window, crying through the lock,
    "Are all the children in their beds?
    It's past eight o'clock!"

254

Good night,
Sleep tight,
Wake up bright
In the morning light,
To do what's right
With all your might.

Hush-a-bye, baby, on the treetop,
When the wind blows, the cradle will rock;
When the bough breaks, the cradle will fall,
And down will come baby, cradle and all.

Diddle, diddle, dumpling, my son John
Went to bed with his trousers on!
One shoe off and one shoe on,
Diddle, diddle, dumpling, my son John.

Hush little baby, don't say a word,
Papa's going to buy you a mockingbird.

And if that mockingbird won't sing,
Papa's going to buy you a diamond ring.

And if that diamond ring turns brass,
Papa's going to buy you a looking glass.

And if that looking glass gets broke,
Papa's going to buy you a billy goat.

And if that billy goat won't pull,
Papa's going to buy you a cart and bull.

And if that cart and bull fall down,
You'll still be the sweetest little baby in town.